Daniel Brako is a graduate of Newcastle University, where he studied psychology and philosophy.

After working in the mental health field, he decided to pursue a literary career, embracing his love of screenplays and novels. Inclined to blend fantasy, thriller and metaphysical elements, his books include *Christos*, *Cubeology*, and *Doors*.

Daniel lives in Sydney, Australia.

For more information visit www.danielbrako.com

I0631008

First published by Momentum in 2013
This edition published in 2013 by Momentum
Pan Macmillan Australia Pty Ltd
1 Market Street, Sydney 2000

A CIP record for this book is available at the National Library of
Australia

Doors

EPUB format: 9781743342091
Mobi format: 9781743342107
Print on Demand format: 9781743342114

Cover design by Matt O'Keefe
Edited by Gareth Beal
Proofread by Jason Nahrung

Macmillan Digital Australia: www.macmillandigital.com.au

To report a typographical error, please visit momentumbooks.com.au/
contact/

Visit www.momentumbooks.com.au to read more about all our books and
to buy books online.

DOORS

Daniel Brako

momentum

PROLOGUE

RUN

The city park was lush and sprawling, making it an ideal place to hide. David Druas removed his jacket and dumped it behind some bushes. After rolling up his shirtsleeves, the thirty-five-year-old psychologist rejoined a nearby path, adopting a leisurely stroll. On this spring day, anonymity was everything.

Pedestrians were scattered everywhere, like sprinkles on a green cake. As David joined their ranks, he stole a glance over his shoulder. There was no sign of pursuit.

A bird sang joyously before fluttering away.

Determined to remain incognito, David approached a teenager. "Hey buddy, I'll give you twenty bucks for your cap."

The teen glowered. "Do I look like a salesman to you?"

David withdrew forty dollars from an envelope. "Sun's a little bright, is all."

"Tell it to someone who gives a shit."

"I'm telling you." David withdrew another sixty. "Do we have a deal?"

Greed lit the teen's oily face. "We do now." He took the cash and surrendered his cap. It had two sentences written on it: *Jesus is coming. Hide the porn.*

David pulled the cap low over his eyes and moved on. It was difficult to estimate how much time had passed since escaping, because fear had a tendency to expand each second, impregnating the mind with distortions. By now his description would have been circulated to every law enforcer within the district.

While trying to get his bearings, David passed a toilet block that had three doors. Two of the doors were wooden with standard gender logos and peeling beige paint. The third door, wedged awkwardly between them, appeared to be made out of misshapen metal. David had no idea what lay behind it. Instead of pausing to find out, he quickened his pace, stealing deeper into the park.

Considered a safe place, the park was frequented by parents with small children. David ambled toward a woman struggling with a pram and several shopping parcels. "It seems we share a passion, you and I."

The woman eyed him with suspicion. "Excuse me?"

"Shopping! Just this morning my boyfriend warned me he's going to cancel my subscription to *Stylus Weekly* if I max out another credit card." David rolled his eyes. "And he calls *me* a drama queen."

"My husband's exactly the same, only he uses guilt tactics." She laughed. "It never works."

David flashed his best smile. "From one shopper to another, can I help you carry those bags?"

The woman, whose name ironically turned out to be Grace, handed over a bunch of designer-label bags. They were surprisingly heavy. Falling into step with each other, they continued along the path. When they eventually passed a park ranger, he appeared oblivious to them. They were, after all, just another couple in a sea of many.

As a clinical psychologist, it was David's job to talk to people. Conversation was an essential tool, not unlike a painter's brush. He and Grace canvassed various topics, allowing those expanded seconds to pass a little more easily.

"Newton went mad at least twice during his life."

"Sir Isaac Newton? The famous scientist?"

David nodded. "Depression, anxiety, insomnia, delusions of persecution … the guy was borderline psychotic. It was probably self-induced."

"How?"

As they rounded a bend in the path David spotted two police officers strategically positioned near a fountain. Unlike the park ranger, they were alert and watchful. They were also armed.

"David?"

David turned to Grace.

"How was Newton's madness self-induced?"

"Through mercury poisoning, most likely." David considered turning back, but that would draw attention. He inched closer to his sham wife.

"I suspect my brother-in-law's depression is self-induced," Grace said. "Not through mercury, but booze …"

Oblivious to the situation, Grace began a running commentary of her family's shortcomings. David did his best to respond, trying to appear carefree. As they drew closer to the fountain, he kept reminding himself that the cops were searching for a single fugitive, not a family man.

With no raised guns or crackling tasers, the charade appeared to be working. Just another couple in a sea of many. But then David unwittingly made eye contact with the female officer. He knew her. Judging by her startled expression, the realization was mutual.

"It's him!" she yelled. "It's Druas!"

Dropping the designer bags, David turned and fled.

"What the hell?!" Grace protested.

There was no time to apologize to his sham wife.

Running was all that mattered.

Running was his only hope.

THE PAGE

"Running the four-minute mile was an unachievable dream. Everyone believed that until a man named Roger Bannister achieved it." David filled a glass with water and handed it to his client, a computer programmer named Eugene. "But what happened next was even more amazing."

David's office, located thirty floors above street level, was drenched in sunlight. Wall-to-ceiling windows provided staggering views of the city.

"What happened next?"

"Well, that's the strange thing. You'd think that Bannister's new record would have been difficult to break. Immensely difficult. But within one year it had been broken dozens of times."

"How is that possible?"

"It all comes down to belief, Eugene." David tapped the side of his head. "When you break the conceptual barrier, the impossible—"

The office door opened and a disheveled man stormed in. He was followed by Celeste, David's secretary.

"I'm sorry, Dr Druas." Celeste blushed. "I tried to stop him."

It took David a few moments to recognize the newcomer. "Hans?"

Hans's eyes, lifeless portals to a withered soul, were glazed. "She didn't want me to talk to you. Your pretty secretary. She said I needed to make an appointment."

Celeste stepped toward David's desk, hovering near the phone. "Should I call security?"

David shook his head. "I think we can handle this in-house."

"I didn't know where else to go," Hans admitted. "They're everywhere."

David turned to his scheduled client. "Would you mind if we end today's session a little earlier than usual, Eugene? Celeste will book you a complimentary replacement."

"Sounds good to me, doc."

Celeste and Eugene departed. Sunlight and tension remained.

"They're everywhere." Hans glanced toward a framed Escher reproduction, hanging on a pastel wall.

"Who's everywhere?"

"Enigmas that no one else can see."

David was concerned. The man standing before him, Hans Werner, had been a sporadic client for the past twelve months. The overworked and underpaid accountant suffered from stress and low self-esteem. He had no history of mental illness.

"Would you like to sit down, Hans, so that we can talk more comfortably?"

"Do you believe in God, Dr Druas?"

"I'm interested in hearing *your* thoughts and beliefs."

"Don't bullshit me, doctor!" Hans wrenched the picture off the wall, smashing its frame against a bookshelf. Glass fragments littered the floor. "Do you or don't you believe in God?"

David hesitated. "I believe in the possibility."

The response seemed to sap Hans of anger. "I believed every day of my life, until the abominations started."

"Abominations?"

"At first I thought they were gifts from God. But gifts don't bring pain."

David stepped closer to his client, traversing the glass shards. "Hans, what abominations?"

"The doors." Hans nodded toward the pastel wall. "There's one right there."

"You can see a door etched onto this wall?"

"It's not etched on. It's real." Hans approached the wall, using his hand to sketch out a rectangular shape. "This particular one's made of a light-colored wood, like ash. Plain and simple."

"If that were true, Hans, wouldn't I be able to see the door?"

"You have to invoke the doors before you can see them."

"How does a person invoke doors?"

"Is that what you want?" Hans's German accent was thick with hope. "Do you want to invoke the doors?"

"I want to understand you, so that I can help. That's why you came here, isn't it?"

Hans withdrew a folded slip of paper from his pocket. "What you're asking me is written on this page." When David reached for the paper, Hans snatched it away. "Once you view the instructions, you can never unview them. Are you sure you want to read what the paper says?"

David extended his open palm.

Time fell still as the two men stood frozen like statues. When Hans eventually surrendered the slip of paper, he moved with the heaviness of marble. David read the instructions.

To invoke the elegance of the doors, begin with what is at hand. Do this literally by cutting a rectangle, otherwise known as a blood symbol, into your palm. Face north and say: Hic et illic, Januae, vos advoco. Touch the blood symbol to the earth, then face east and say: Magnae et parvae, Januae, vos saluto. Touch the blood symbol to the earth, then face south and say: Intus et foras, Januae, vobis credo. Touch the blood symbol to the earth, then face west and say: Nunc et tunc, Januae, vos honoro. Touch the blood symbol to the earth, then say: His verbis et actis pactum consigno.

"Did you find this on the internet?"

Hans shook his head.

"Then where?"

"It was in Matilda."

"Matilda?" David frowned. "Is Matilda the name of a book? A diary?"

"Matilda is a doll. I bought her from the antiques fair."

David recalled Hans's unusual hobby. "You bought the doll – Matilda – to restore her?"

Hans nodded. "I found it tucked away inside her chest. It was a secret never meant to be found."

"What if the opposite were true?"

"How so?"

"Maybe someone was using the doll as a time capsule. A bored teenager, perhaps, with a credit in Latin and a penchant for self-harm." David paused. "Hans, I want you to consider the possibility that these words are someone's idea of a prank."

Hans shook his head. "The words are real. The *consequences* are real."

"You believe the consequences are real because you see these … doors?"

"You think I'm crazy."

"Creative, maybe, but not crazy." David smiled reassuringly. "Have I ever told you about the man who beat cancer?" Hans was silent. "This man, let's call him Carl, was diagnosed with cancer decades ago. When his doctor prescribed an experimental drug, the cancer went into remission."

"Why are you telling me this?"

"Because, like you, Carl made an unexpected discovery. Unfortunately, his discovery caused a relapse."

Hans frowned. "What did he discover?"

David gestured for patience. "When his doctor prescribed a stronger drug, the cancer again went into remission. But fate can be devious. A second discovery, similar to the first, saw Carl's cancer return. It ultimately claimed his life."

"Dr Druas, what did Carl discover?"

"In both instances he discovered that his experimental wonder drugs were placebos. This is a *true* story of a man who cured himself of cancer – not once, but twice – using the power of his mind."

"That invocation you're holding isn't a placebo."

"Not in a traditional sense. But what if, like a sugar pill, it has led to changes in your perception?" David paused. "You feel trapped in an inescapable cycle because a false seed is germinating in your mind. I can help you root out that seed."

"Seed?" Hans laughed. There was no joy in that hollow sound. "I'd say it's more like a tree."

"Then together you and I will chop it down."

"If you could see what I've seen, you wouldn't be so sure of yourself." Hans lowered his voice to a whisper. "I've died, Dr Druas. I've *literally* died and been reborn."

As David studied his client, an accountant clothed in agony, something became apparent. Words were insufficient for this particular number cruncher. What Hans needed was something quantifiable, something tangible, to persuade him.

David approached his desk and took out a silver letter opener. It was shaped like a gargoyle, with a spike protruding from its mouth.

"What are you doing?"

"Helping you cut down that tree of yours." David cut a small rectangle into his palm.

The invocation of the doors had begun.

INVOKING DOORS

Sunlight glinted off the silver letter opener as David wiped his blood from its tip.

"Are you sure you want to do this?" Hans asked.

"Absolutely. It's tree choppin' season." Ignoring his stinging palm, David turned to face north. "Hic et illic, Januae, vos advoco …"

The invocation was a simple ritual. As David progressed through each step, he wondered if it had once been a child's game. Perhaps a victim of sadistic modifications. Aside from the self-mutilation, there was a whimsical aspect to it all.

Brevity was another of its charms. In less than a minute the ritual was over. As David lifted his palm from the carpet, he noticed that a blood stain had been left behind. Four blood stains in total. He idly wondered if they would be easy to remove. The throbbing lingered.

"How do you feel?" Hans wanted to know.

David shrugged. "I feel unchanged. Like I said earlier, Hans, the invocation is a prank."

Hans glanced beyond David's shoulder. "Look at the wall behind you."

The wall in question, according to Hans's earlier claim, contained a concealed door that became visible after performing the ritual. A superstitious man might have been afraid to look, but David Druas was a man of science.

***

When Hans sought out David for help, he never expected him to invoke the doors. Psychologists were supposed to be measured. They were supposed to be Zen-like listeners who floated on a sea of rational thinking. That's why people paid them. Invoking the doors, Hans now knew, was anything but measured. It was messing with the Devil's delights.

Four weeks had passed since Hans first encountered the doors. He remembered dismantling Matilda, finding the slip of paper hidden within her Victorian chest, and being perplexed by its instructions. He also remembered the ensuing questions: was it a game, a gift from God, a trick from the Devil? There was only one way to find out. That was the night his life changed, the night the concealed doors lost their concealment.

Now, as he stood in this sun-drenched office, the doors were once again being invoked. A small part of Hans wanted to stop the madness from unfolding, but the larger part wanted the ritual to occur. He needed someone to share the nightmare with.

"How do you feel?" Hans asked once the ritual was over.

"I feel unchanged." David rambled on.

Hans glanced at the strange wooden door. "Look at the wall behind you."

David obliged.

"Well?" Hans held his breath. "What do you see?"

Seconds flitted by as David studied the wall. "Truth is heavier than gold. And more costly."

"I can bear the truth. It's all I've ever wanted."

When David turned back, it was obvious that something was wrong. His face should have been filled with awe. Or shock. Or fear. Instead it held only commiseration. "I don't see anything, Hans. I don't see anything other than a blank wall."

The words were hard to digest. They hurt unexpectedly, like a stab to the stomach. "Are you sure? Are you absolutely sure?"

David nodded.

"But that doesn't make any sense."

"Actually, when you look at it from a logical perspective, it makes perfect sense. The ritual is a hoax."

Hans shook his head. "You must have done something wrong."

"You saw me perform each step. You heard me speak each word. I followed the instructions precisely. What does that suggest to you?"

Insanity. The chilling possibility slivered into Hans's brain, coiling itself into a tight knot. He laughed involuntarily, fearing he was a few trees short of a forest.

"Hans?"

"I'm not insane!" He yelled to silence any doubt.

"I never said you were. *Confused* is perhaps a better descriptor."

Confused. Crazy. They were different ends of the same stick. Psychology couldn't help him because the problem at hand was an otherworldly enigma. It was greater than the human mind could comprehend.

DEPARTURES

"Goodbye, Dr Druas." Hans lumbered toward the exit.

"If you leave, I won't be able to help you."

"You can't help me if I stay."

David grabbed Hans's arm, forcing him to stop. "Let me try."

The two men locked eyes. Although standing side by side, there was an unfathomable distance between them.

"Your attempt failed." Yanking free of David's grip, Hans stormed through the doorway that every man, woman and skeptic could see.

Celeste, seated at her reception desk, flinched.

"Please wait …" David followed Hans into the sky-scraper's public-access hallway, imploring him to rethink his decision. It was to no avail. When the elevator opened, announced by a corresponding ping, Hans entered.

"Help is dead, Dr Druas." He grimaced. "So is truth."

The silver doors closed, barring further discussion, as the elevator spirited Hans away.

"Shit!" David trudged back to his office.

"He flew the coop?" Celeste ran a brush through her auburn hair.

"The coop couldn't contain him." David scanned the empty reception area. "I thought I was booked out today."

"You were, but I canceled a few of your appointments to make space for Mr Werner." Celeste lowered her brush and retrieved her purse. "Your next client will be here in forty minutes. Luckily for you I can squeeze my lunch break into thirty."

"You're a gem."

"Today and always." Celeste departed.

Reentering his sunlit office, David realized his own appetite was nonexistent, withered by the specter of failure. He began plucking glass shards from the smashed frame, depositing them into the dustbin. Cleaning relaxed the mind.

As he progressed, taking care not to cut himself, David glimpsed something at the edge of his vision. When he turned his gaze toward the rectangular oddity, disbelief and horror collided, unhinging reality as he knew it.

A door, made out of pale wood, was superimposed onto the pastel wall. It lingered there, unassumingly, as though it had always existed. Of course, in a world governed by stable laws of physics, that otherworldly door couldn't exist. And yet there it was, happily flaunting the rules.

David snapped his eyes shut and counted to twenty. When he opened his eyes, the door remained. It looked so real that he was tempted to interact with it. But that wasn't an option. Psychologists were supposed to *treat* delusions. They were supposed to see the world through clear and unbiased eyes.

"Get a grip!" he told himself.

Was this iatrogenesis, the creation of a disorder by an attempt to treat it? Or was some other psychopathology at play? David began pacing the room, ransacking his mind for answers that refused to be found. With each circuit he stole regular glimpses at the pale door. A psychologist contemplating his own psychosis – what would Freud say?

Celeste's voice pierced the silence. "What are you doing, David?"

David stopped pacing. Although his rational mind cautioned against yielding to the hallucination, he had to ask the obvious question. "Do you see it?"

Celeste frowned. "See what?"

David pointed at the pale door.

Celeste studied the wall, her frown deepening. "What am I meant to be looking at?"

Frustration clawed at David's chest. He thought of Hans. "You don't see anything unusual?"

"The wall could do with a fresh coat of paint. Pastels are like that. Oh, and your Escher picture is missing." Her eyes settled on the broken frame.

David felt a spike of anger, although he couldn't decide who or what he was angry with. "Why did you come back? I thought you were going to lunch."

"I've been at lunch for the past half hour. David, are you feeling all right?"

He offered a smile to ease her concern. It felt unsteady on his face. "Time escaped me."

"Should I wait a few minutes before sending in your next client?"

"Actually, can you cancel all of my appointments? I know it's late notice, but something unexpected has come up."

"Do you need me to call someone for you? A doctor? Professor Milner, perhaps?"

"I just need you to free up my schedule." David ushered Celeste toward the *other* office door. "When you're done, why not take the rest of the day off? I'll see you tomorrow." He gave her a final smile before closing the door between them.

After considering his options David returned to the white door. It was like a bewitching siren, albeit one with corners rather than curves. Placing his misgivings aside, he cautiously reached for the unknown. Unlike the pastel wall, the door felt smooth and cold to the touch. It was a refreshing burst.

Hallucinations, although dangerous to engage with, could provide insights into the subconscious mind. What would this door reveal? David grasped the perfectly round knob, which was also made out of pale wood, and gently opened the door. It gave with a faint tearing sound, similar to that of a hermetic seal being broken.

David goggled at the surreal vista that lay before him.

It beckoned.

THE FOREST

A forest lay beyond the pale door. Was the hallucination deepening, or was Hans Werner correct? Bracing himself for either possibility, David stepped through the doorway.

For a heart-pounding moment, blackness consumed everything. As ear pressure spiked, up and down became indistinguishable from left and right. Fortunately, the pain and disorientation ended when he emerged from the doorway, stumbling onto moist soil.

The air was tangy and humid, unlike the air-conditioned office that remained visible through the freestanding door behind him. David unbuttoned his shirt, ignoring the perspiration building at his temples, and scanned the environment.

Anorexic trees were everywhere. With a diameter of roughly eight inches, and a height approaching forty feet, they were incredibly thin and tall. Lacking branches, their gray trunks reached up toward a magenta sky and ended in a thick mass of golden leaves.

"Where am I?" David wondered aloud.

Unlike other forests David had seen, this one was devoid of ground litter. Its soil was black.

Stretching out in every direction, the forest was an explorer's dream. After affirming the door's location in his mind, David cautiously set off through the trees. Aside from the breeze that occasionally rustled the canopy, silence and stillness prevailed.

A small clearing offered an unrestricted view of the sky, revealing two moons. One was large, the other was tiny. They floated in the magenta sky like fruit floating in alcoholic punch. It was an intoxicating sight.

Hoping to ascertain the planet's authenticity, David decided to take some samples of the place. After moving out of the clearing, he began to dig. The black soil smelled moldy, but not unpleasant. He suspected it must be hiding an impressive root system to prevent the trees from toppling. Either that or the normal laws of physics didn't apply.

A golden blur of movement startled David, elevating his heartbeat. Perhaps it was time to leave the silent forest and return home. After placing a handful of soil into his pocket, David noticed a tiny creature watching him. No longer than ten inches, it resembled a mouse lemur with dirty yellow fur.

Rustling from the canopy revealed more yellow and gold creatures, scurrying through the leaves. A few descended to the ground and studied David with bulbous eyes. Their ringleader, the first creature to have revealed itself, inched closer.

"I won't hurt you." David extended his hand toward the newcomer.

The creature crept forward, sniffing the soil-covered fingers. Displaying a boldness far greater than its size, it leaped onto David's shoulder and began sniffing his hair and clothes. Each footstep tickled unexpectedly.

When David petted the creature, it began clicking. Uncertainty evaporated from the onlookers as several scampered forward to begin their own investigations. David laughed as they sprang onto him, their tiny paws nudging skin and fabric alike. The musical clicks swelled in a joyous chorus.

Numerous creatures now filled the golden canopy, attracted by the sound. David hoped they wouldn't all descend otherwise he'd be swamped. Their enthusiasm was becoming a little disconcerting.

One creature, missing part of its left ear, bit his arm.

"Aoww!" David flicked the culprit away. Outraged, it responded with a sequence of shrill and sharp clicks. This would-be battle call quickly spread, replacing the song of friendship. Two more of the creatures bit into his flesh.

"Stop it. Get off!" David shook himself free, dislodging all of the creatures. This only seemed to unsettle them further. Their shrill clicking echoed through the trees, drawing reinforcements. The forest was silent no longer.

Massively outnumbered, David turned and fled. As he raced through the forest, creatures sprang onto him, dropping from the canopy like spiders from a web. Their tiny fangs kept piercing his flesh.

The forest whirled and David stumbled, hitting his head on one of the trees. For a few seconds a peaceful daze engulfed him. He was unaware of the creatures piling onto his prone body, until he felt their fangs again. Although it was difficult to stand up, he staggered forward, drawn by the pale door that lingered in the distance.

As the creatures escalated their attack, blood mixed readily with sweat and black dirt. David blocked out the pain, rushing ahead through the pale door. As before, there was a brief period of darkness, roaring ear pressure, and disorientation. Ignoring these effects, David emerged into his office and slammed the door shut behind him.

It took him a few seconds to realize something was amiss. Despite the frenzied attack, there was no blood, no bite marks, and no squawking creatures. There was no evidence whatsoever to corroborate what had happened.

Burying his face in his hands, David sank to the floor. He couldn't afford to have another breakdown. The last one had been costly enough, inadvertently caused by an aspiring actor named Avan Singh.

AVAN SINGH (PAST)

Avan Singh stood on the stage, dressed like the Sheriff of Nottingham. The only other person present was the director.

"Friar Tuck's got all the best lines." Avan quoted his favorite. "'Altruism isn't dead, it's just demented.'"

"You lookin' to swap roles?"

"Not unless you offer me *the Hood*." Avan wondered why the lead role had gone to a female. In their modernized version of the play, she stole from the rich and kept the spoils for herself and her merry men. "Maybe I should just arrest that slut and be done with it."

"Firstly, Robin Hood is not a slut – she's a sultry thief. There's a difference. Secondly, if you arrested her, we wouldn't have a story."

Avan disagreed. "A jail stint is still a story."

"The audience don't want four walls and defeat. They want drama. They want bows and bloody arrows."

A creaking door announced the arrival of a newcomer to the theater.

"What an audience *really* wants is love." Avan excitedly gestured for David to join them on the stage.

"Love?" The director cast a glance toward David, before jabbing Avan in the ribs.

"Aoww!" Avan complained. "What was that for?"

The director grinned. "No reason. I'll leave you to your … guest."

"Where are you going?"

"To the hardware store. We need more fake grass." The director made his exit through a thicket of plywood trees.

Avan smiled as David mounted the stage. "Welcome to Sherwood Forest."

"Forget Sherwood. Look at you – an Indian-born Sheriff of Nottingham."

"You should see who we've got to play Robin Hood."

"I read the flyer. It's a memorable cast." David eyed Avan's tunic. "And dapper to boot. Who's your tailor?"

"*Fancy-dress-n-Frankenstein.* They give us a 75% discount, we give them first dibs on any unsold tickets."

"Very enterprising."

"We have a similar deal with the local hardware store." Avan nodded toward the plywood trees, many of which still needed painting.

"So what brings you to Nottinghamshire?"

"I was hoping to catch one of your rehearsals." David scanned the empty theater. "Where is everyone?"

"We finished early. Little John had a dental appointment."

"Oh." David looked disappointed.

"Since you came all this way, why don't you join me for dinner? My treat."

David hesitated. "I don't want to impose."

"Trust me, there's no danger of that. Just give me a minute to change into something a little less … dapper."

***

Although Avan's apartment proved to be small, it was big on color. The walls, the paintings, the cushions on the sofa: everything was rich and exotic. David felt like he was in a Bollywood movie.

"You live here by yourself?"

"Me and William Shakespeare."

"William Shakespeare?"

Avan nodded toward a colorful macaw. "What would you like to drink?"

"Whatever you're having." David studied the elderly parrot. He looked proudly regal, despite viewing the world through metal bars.

Avan handed David a beer. "He loves music. Why don't you play him something?"

"A music-loving macaw?" David chose The Beatles from a nearby CD collection.

"The man's got good taste in music." Avan began pulling ingredients out of the pantry.

David stepped through into the kitchen. "How can I help?"

"Can you dice onions?"

"Where's the chopping board?"

***

After dinner the pair found themselves on the sofa, relaxing among the colorful cushions.

"I think it's time for a toast."

"Another one?" David eyed his vodka, trying to remember when spirits had replaced ale. "You know, I don't usually fraternize with clients."

"I'm not a *client*." Avan spurned the word. "You banished my demons months ago."

"So what are we toasting this time?"

Avan considered the question. "New beginnings."

"To new beginnings."

After clicking their glasses together, David found himself turning away from Avan's intense gaze, wishing the lounge was less cozy.

"What a perfect night." Avan caressed David's cheek.

David pulled away. "Don't spoil things."

"How do you know this won't *enhance* things?"

"Believe me, I know."

"How?" Avan persisted.

"The same way I know I wouldn't enjoy sex with a toothless, ninety-year-old woman."

"Am I that repulsive?"

"Of course not." David regretted his drunken analogy. "You're an amazing person."

"Then why won't you give us a chance?"

"Because there is no *us*. I've told you before: I'm not gay."

Silence engulfed the room, bleaching the color away.

"In the theater, we're taught to look beyond appearances. We're taught to go to a deeper place because an actor can't choose who he or she is paired with. Try an exercise with me."

"Sexual orientation can't be altered, Avan."

"I'm not asking you to alter anything. I'm just asking you to liberate your mind."

David put his vodka aside. "What do you want me to do?"

"Stand up." Avan did the same, placing his hands on David's shoulders to square him up. "Now, close your eyes. This exercise is all about exploring the senses. Tell me, David, what do you hear?" It was a simple enough question.

"I hear music playing. Cars outside. A mechanical hum – is that the fridge?" There was no response. "I just heard myself swallow. I can hear you snickering. Softly."

Avan took David's hand and guided it. "What do you feel?"

"I feel the smoothness of your hair." As David ran his fingers through Avan's shoulder-length curls, he found himself thinking about Celeste. She had beautiful hair. "It feels thick and lush. I want the name of your shampoo," he joked.

"Focus. What do you smell?"

His voice was soft and close. David shifted uncomfortably. "I smell you."

"What do I smell like?"

"Mostly Malibu."

"What else?"

"Curry spice. Cinnamon." It was an exotic blend. "And a hint of something else. Musk, maybe?"

"What do you taste?"

Although David could guess what was about to happen, he flinched when Avan's mouth pressed against his own. After a moment's hesitation, David parted his lips, allowing Avan's tongue to enter like a key turning in a lock. The sweet taste of Malibu was unmistakable. But the experience was less about taste and more about exploration. Their tongues pressed heavily against each other, seeking oneness. When David pulled away and opened his eyes, he saw that Avan had an erection.

"What was it like for you?" Avan asked.

David didn't have an erection. He wasn't even semi-hard. "I'm sorry."

"Sorry?" Resentment flooded Avan's eyes. "Sorry that I don't have a cunt?"

"Goodbye, Avan." David walked away from the colorful apartment, stepping into the dark night.

PROOF

After visiting the anorexic forest, David wrote two words in his diary: *Cause + Effect.* Governing the entire universe, causality was an inescapable principle. And yet he had seemingly escaped it. Despite being attacked by the clicking creatures, his injuries, the effects, were nonexistent. It defied logic.

Putting his diary aside, David contemplated the setting sun. It lit the skyline in hues of red and orange, reminding him of the magenta sky that existed beyond the pale door. Blocking out the memory, he turned to the artificial colors of his computer screen and opened the client database. It was time to make a house call.

***

As David drove, he spotted an assortment of otherworldly doors. They seemed to be randomly placed, infusing the city with unexpected colors and forms. A glowing amethyst door, nestled in a preschool fence, proved so disconcerting that he almost veered off the road. It was a relief when the car's navigation system eventually announced, "You have reached your destination."

The townhouse looked cold and uninviting. David rang the doorbell.

After a few moments the door opened. "You shouldn't be here," Hans glared. "You never make house calls."

"Normally, no. But normalcy died today."

Hans noticed a man in a brown suit loitering across the street.

"Nosy neighbors used to be discreet," David joked.

"He's no neighbor of mine." Hans grimaced. "Why are you here, Dr Druas?"

David inhaled deeply. "Because I see the doors too."

"It worked!" Hans opened the door fully, inviting David into the gloom.

***

Prior to his visit, David imagined Hans's house as being clean and orderly. As he sat across from the accountant, sipping tap water from a cracked china mug, he realized the opposite was true. Everything was in disarray.

"I don't understand what's happening, but I assume it's a form of psychosis."

"You're not sick, Dr Druas. Neither of us are."

David lowered his drink and raised his arms. "No bite marks."

"That's how it works. The doors heal travelers."

"Travelers?"

"Anyone capable of stepping through them."

David shook his head. "The doors aren't real."

"But we've *both* seen them."

"Shared delusions, although rare, have been documented." David paused. "Tell me something, Hans: in all your travels, have you ever brought back any proof?"

Hans remained silent.

"I didn't think so."

"The doors are cunning, Dr Druas. They don't let you bring anything back."

"What you're doing right now is called *compensating*. You're manufacturing excuses to fit the fantasy." David paused. "If we apply Ockham's razor, the fantasy falls apart."

"You're wrong." Hans stepped over a slumbering Alsatian to retrieve some stationery.

"What's that you're writing?" David asked.

"The blunting of Ockham's razor." Hans sealed the note in an envelope and handed it to David. "Different doors lead to different locations. I've jotted down the details of a door on Maple Street, a few miles south of here."

David began to open the envelope.

"Not yet! Open it *after* you've visited the door yourself. That way—"

"I can compare my experiences with your experiences to test for consistency?"

Hans nodded.

"An elegant solution to a perplexing problem." David placed the envelope in his pocket and made ready to leave.

"Promise me one thing, Dr Druas: after you visit there, promise me you'll never step through another door again. They're too dangerous to play with."

"I thought you said the doors were safe?"

Hans avoided his gaze. "Not all injuries are physical."

David saw a man who was beaten, broken and fragile. The doors looming across the city were to blame.

***

David reached Maple Street around midnight. He purposely chose that time because fewer people were about, reducing the likelihood of being seen. Fortunately it didn't take long to find his objective.

The local music store, it turned out, had a regular door for customers. It also had an otherworldly door for travelers. This second door was made from exotic animal skins, and felt like suede.

When David opened the door, he heard the familiar tearing sound. The colorful vista that awaited him, however, was unexpected. He hurried forward, once again encountering a moment of darkness and disorientation, before emerging into a crystalline realm.

A blue ground, made from a bedrock of solid crystal, lay beneath a jade sky. Gigantic crystals jutted up from the ground at random intervals, infusing additional colors into the environment, like a natural kaleidoscope. It was heaven spliced with perfection.

Unlike the anorexic forest, the large open spaces made an ambush unlikely; nevertheless David remained cautious as he abandoned the animal-skin doorway, stepping toward the nearest crystal outgrowth.

"Beautiful …" More than four times his height, this particular crystal was mostly clear, like quartz, with occasional streaks of apricot. It felt cool and hard to the touch, not unlike crystals from Earth. David couldn't tell if it was the land's coolness, its colors, or the solitude, but he wished he could bathe in such beauty forever.

***

When David reemerged onto Maple Street, it was with a sense of regret. No man willingly abandoned heaven. Of course, staying in the crystalline realm indefinitely simply wasn't an option. Life needed to continue.

While fingering Hans Werner's letter, David realized he was being watched by the same man who had been loitering near Hans Werner's house.

"What do you want?" David yelled across the street, furious at being followed.

Ignoring the question, the man in the brown suit began strolling away.

"Hey!" David chased after him.

The man ambled into an alley. David followed seconds later but his quarry was nowhere to be seen, lost to the night.

PERCEPTION

"To perceive is to sample life's wonders." Professor Olivia Milner addressed the packed lecture hall. "Nevertheless, perception is a subjective experience because it hinges on the *interpretation* of sensory input. Take this painting by Salvador Dali, for example."

The projector flashed *Slave Market with the Disappearing Bust of Voltaire* (1940) onto the wall. "If we look near the center of the image, we find a reversible figure. There are two nuns framed in an arch. Simultaneously there is the bust of Voltaire – a philosopher critical of the Catholic church." She paused. "A single visual stimulus can potentially result in radically different perceptions. We'll discuss this more next time, when we study the roles of expectation and past experiences."

As the students began to file out, a former student approached her.

"I thought it was you sneaking in toward the end of the lecture." She embraced David warmly. "No clients today?"

"I took the day off. The whole week, actually." He smiled. "Perhaps I can tell you about it over a bite to eat?"

Olivia knew David well enough to know something was amiss. His smile, like the Dali, held mixed meanings.

***

The college gardens provided a serene getaway from campus life. Sitting on a stone bench, Olivia ate fruit salad while David picked at a shepherd's pie.

They first met more than a decade ago, when he was enrolled as an undergraduate at the university. In those early days, David was an apathetic student. After his mother was diagnosed with dementia, however, psychology took on a new relevance. It became a lifeline, propelling him from average to exceptional. When he began postgraduate studies, Olivia elected to be his supervisor. Despite a rocky start, David Druas was arguably one of her favorite and most gifted students.

"How's the pie?" she asked.

"It's okay."

"And the man eating the pie? Is he okay too?"

David placed the pie aside. "If I tell you something, something that sounds entirely unbelievable, will you promise to keep an open mind?"

"Hand on heart."

"A client of mine, Hans Werner, came to my office yesterday—"

"Are we divulging names now?"

"Breaching client confidentiality is the least of my concerns." David provided a detailed description of the past twenty-four hours. It was a glut of information that left Olivia both chilled and numb. At the end of it all he asked, "What do you think?"

Despite more than forty years of studying psychology, seeking to unlock the mind and all of its secrets, Olivia was speechless. David was like a son to her. "The note that Hans Werner wrote, do you still have it?"

David handed her a note, written in an unfamiliar scrawl. *Door = animal skins. World = colored crystals rising from a blue crystal ground. Green sky.* <u>*Perfection*</u>.

"And the original invocation?" Olivia asked.

"That's in my office safe. What do you make of it all?"

Olivia hesitated. "We both know you have a heavy workload. Being exposed to so many clients, so many *unwell* clients, exacts a toll."

"You're speaking from a scientific perspective. But the doors defy science."

"People who see goblins and unicorns would argue the same point."

"I can *prove* my point."

"How?"

"There's a door only a few minutes from here. Watch me step through it."

"I'm not sure that's a good idea."

"Open mind, Olivia – you promised."

Olivia considered her options. "I'll give you the benefit of the doubt, on one condition."

"Name it."

"If you fail, I want you to seek medical evaluation and treatment."

David nodded. "Whatever you say."

***

Olivia and David strolled toward one of the largest buildings on campus.

"Why have you brought me to the library?"

"We're not going inside." David began skirting the perimeter. "I spotted a door on my way to visit you."

"Do you mind if I film this?" Rather than documenting a miracle, Olivia wanted to gather psychiatric evidence in case David reneged on their agreement.

"Go for it." After approaching an unremarkable section of wall, he faced the camera phone. "For the record, my name is David Druas. I'm about to enter a glass door that no one else can see."

Olivia watched closely as he pretended to open the door. Her screen turned to static. "Just a moment, David. I'm having problems with my phone."

"It doesn't matter. I don't think I can go in there."

"Why?" The fantasy, she believed, was unraveling.

"It looks sweltering. There are fires everywhere. Most of the ground is on fire."

"Are you looking into hell? Is that what you see?"

"No." David pretended to close the door. "Hell is being judged by skeptics."

He looked so wounded, Olivia scarcely noticed the static had ceased.

***

Ten minutes later, Olivia and David were standing outside an average-looking house. They had found their current location by randomly strolling through neighboring streets.

"What do you see?"

"An amber door. Come on."

"Trespassing is an offense, David."

"I'm not going to enter the actual house."

Against her better judgment, Olivia began filming as she followed David in through the front gate.

David turned to the camera. "My name is David Druas and I'm about to enter a hidden amber door. This is not a trick."

As he pretended to open the door, Olivia noted the gesture again coincided with the appearance of static.

"David—"

"This world looks safe."

He stepped toward the house's exterior wall and …

Olivia turned the page of her textbook. It was massive in size, and boring in content. Although she'd been reading it for awhile, each fact seemed to blur into the next. She could scarcely recall what she had read.

Olivia closed the book and switched off her office computer. The work day was over. It was time to go home.

MISSING

Celeste had spent the past week watching daytime television. Her impromptu holiday, the result of Hans Werner's dramatic visit to the office, proved boring and tedious. She was eager to return to work.

Arriving at the office early, she made herself a coffee and began preparing for the day ahead. The first client arrived at 8:55 am. Since David had yet to make an appearance, she phoned his cell. It went to voicemail.

"David, it's Celeste. Just letting you know your 9:00 am has arrived. See you soon." She disconnected the call and turned to the client. "Dr Druas will be arriving any moment. In the meantime, can I get you something to drink?"

As the 9:00 am slot came and went, Celeste struggled to hide her concern. David was always punctual. Dependable. Reliable. He wasn't the sort of person to neglect his responsibilities.

Unable to determine his whereabouts, Celeste began canceling the morning appointments. She apologized to frustrated clients, but her excuses felt insubstantial, not unlike her missing boss.

***

Olivia was preparing lecture notes when her cell phone rang. She extracted it from beneath a pile of papers that littered her desk. "Olivia Milner speaking."

"Professor Milner, this is Celeste Ellewood."

Olivia removed her spectacles. "Good morning, Celeste. How's Hawk?"

"His paw's a lot better. The vet thinks he'll make a full recovery."

"That's wonderful news."

"Better than expected." Celeste paused. "I'm actually calling about David."

"Don't tell me he's injured his paw as well?"

"I wouldn't know. He didn't come in to work this morning." She sounded anxious. "Do you know where he is?"

"I'm afraid not. I haven't seen David since …" Olivia detected a chink in her memory.

"Professor Milner?"

"It was last week sometime. I'm sorry I can't be more exact."

When the conversation ended, Olivia sat in silence. Despite her reputation for being sharp-witted, her memories of David's recent visit were indistinct. She could recall what they ate for lunch, for example, but not what they discussed. It was maddening.

As Olivia lifted her phone, preparing to send a text, she recalled filming David. Since the film's content was unknown to her, she scrolled through the phone's options and played the recording in question.

"My name is David Druas and I'm about to enter a hidden amber door. This is not a trick."

The words unleashed a flood of forgotten memories. Olivia was not only able to recall every detail leading up to that moment, she could also remember walking back to her office afterward. These revelations raised endless questions, but one question towered above the others: What happened to David?

***

Although Lisa Cho preferred being out in the field, she was currently rostered to the station, inundated with boring caseloads. She collected yet another form, snatching it from a voluminous stack, and approached the waiting area.

"Ms Ellewood? Celeste Ellewood?"

An attractive woman stood. "I'm Celeste Ellewood."

"I'm Officer Cho. Please come with me."

Lisa led them to a private room where she scanned Celeste's missing person's report. "Your boss didn't show up to work this morning?"

Celeste nodded.

Although the names and details were constantly changing, Lisa had heard this tale countless times. She lifted her pen and began asking the standard questions: when did you last see him, has he missed work before, did he have any prescheduled appointments? Judging by Celeste's answers, she viewed her boss as a beacon of reliability. Lisa wanted to ask if they were screwing. Instead she settled for, "Have you tried contacting his family and friends?"

"David's mother, his only surviving relative, has dementia. His friends haven't heard from him."

"Have you contacted local hospitals?"

Celeste paled.

Lisa chided herself. "Please, don't be alarmed, Ms Ellewood—"

"Celeste."

"Celeste. People go missing every day, for all sorts of reasons. The good news is that most turn up within twenty-four hours. Chances are you don't need to worry."

"So what happens now?"

"I'll update our database. It can be correlated with other emergency departments."

"That's it?"

"If you like, I can put out a KALOF bulletin to alert local patrols."

"You're not going to search for him?"

"Unless there's evidence of foul play, we just don't have the resources." Lisa flashed a comforting smile. "Try not to worry. Like I said, the odds are in your favor."

Once Celeste had left, Lisa created an electronic report. She typed quickly because her lunch break was already half an hour overdue. Office work was stifling to her soul.

THE MAZE

When David opened the amber door, he saw lush foliage set against a pale blue sky.

"David—"

"This world looks safe."

Before Olivia could protest, he stepped through the doorway, encountering a wave of disorientation. The granite courtyard that awaited him was not only enclosed by towering hedges, it contained an ornate fountain made entirely of vines. Able to pump water, it was literally a living work of art.

While examining the fountain, a rustling of leaves caused David to glance back over his shoulder. To his shock, the courtyard had somehow reconfigured itself, becoming smaller in size. The transformation meant the amber door was now gone.

"No!" David rushed to where the door should have been, frustrated by a hedge blocking his path. Although he tried breaking through it, the vines were as hard as the granite ground on which he stood.

More rustling preceded further changes. The previously enclosed courtyard now had four arched corridors leading in different directions. Ignoring them, David began climbing the hedge. When rustling occurred above his head, the hedge became insurmountable, towering into the sky.

Dropping back to the ground, David headed for the nearest archway, hoping it would lead him back to where the amber door had been. Unfortunately, the further he went, the more disorientated he became. Frequent changes to the maze, indicated by the rustling, only exacerbated the problem.

As he padded deeper into the green nightmare, David spotted benches, statues and more fountains. There were also objects that he couldn't recognize. Astonishingly, everything was made out of vines.

Hours passed, but the amber door remained elusive.

When night eventually descended, the maze turned pitch black, due to an inexplicable absence of stars and satellites. Despite the darkness, the reconfigurations continued. David couldn't see the changes but he could hear them. The rustling knew no end, becoming as inescapable as the vines themselves.

***

David awoke to a pale blue sky and a grumbling stomach. His mouth felt impossibly dry. Although it didn't take too long to find a fountain, the water tasted metallic, causing severe stomach cramps. Every subsequent fountain was the same.

Hiking over the granite ground became a robotic pastime. It numbed David's mind. After several hours lumbering back and forth, a bird broke the monotony, soaring across the pale blue sky.

"It's alive?!"

David raced through the maze, following the vine bird as it streaked toward an unknown destination. His efforts were rewarded minutes later, when he rounded a bend and found a towering castle.

Made entirely out of vines, the castle was an architectural wonder that *should* have been visible from anywhere in the maze. Not wanting to lose it, David hastened forward. He made a conscious effort not to blink, knowing by this time that reconfigurations always occurred out of view.

When David crossed the drawbridge, stepping into an enormous hall, he hollered out, "Hello!" Although his voice should have been absorbed by the foliage, it echoed back, sounding tiny and insignificant.

Moving from room to room, David spotted an array of items. Tables and chairs. Beds and cupboards. Ornaments and baubles. The castle even boasted an assortment of armored knights. Everything was made out of vines, even the paintings on the walls.

The library contained shelves of green books. Made from pressed vines, their pages were strewn with unfamiliar symbols. While examining one of the unreadable books, David heard the rustling of leaves. Expecting to see the library rearranged behind him, he turned and barely avoided the swipe of a sword.

Astonishingly, the attacker was a stiff-limbed knight.

"I seek peace." David slowly backed away. "Friendship."

The knight either didn't understand or wasn't listening. It struck again.

David narrowly avoided the blow. "You don't have to do this."

As before, his words had no effect. The determined knight kept lumbering forward, backing him into a corner.

"Okay, have it your way." David tried toppling the knight, but it was like ramming into a concrete pylon. A fist like a knot of tree roots sent him sliding on his back across the hard green floor.

As the knight lurched forward, David dragged himself woozily to his feet. Ducking under another clumsy sword thrust, he turned and fled the library of unreadable books.

Armored knights roamed the grand castle. Although their movements were sluggish, allowing David to avoid confrontation, he barely avoided the battleaxe hurled at his head.

When David eventually crossed the drawbridge, relief surged through his exhausted body. Minutes later, after hearing leaves rustle, he glanced back and saw the castle was gone. Hedges had taken its place.

***

Days passed.

Suffering from dehydration and starvation, David's health rapidly declined. He tried eating the vines, but they made him vomit blood. There came a point when he could no longer walk.

As he lay slumped on the hard granite, drifting in and out of consciousness, someone leaned over him. The newcomer, possibly a hallucination, wore a brown tailored suit. David tried to catch what the man was saying, but it was impossible to concentrate. His mind, like his emaciated body, felt withered.

Closing his eyes, David Druas took a final breath.

Death claimed him quickly.

OLIVIA MILNER

Olivia Milner was baffled. She was baffled not only by David's disappearance, but by her uncooperative memories of the event. A psychological explanation – one that was neat and tidy, ticking all the appropriate boxes – would have been welcome. But such an explanation was as impossible to find as David himself.

Although amnesia and dementia could both explain disappearing memories, neither could explain disappearing people. So what other explanations were there? Post traumatic stress disorder was one possibility, assuming the inciting incident was sufficiently traumatic, but it didn't explain the static that had disrupted the videos on her cell phone. PTSD, like every other psychological explanation, felt flimsy.

As a practicing Buddhist, happy to embrace alternative ways of thinking, Olivia wondered if there could be something to David's extraordinary claims. An open mind is needed to catch the light of knowledge, she often told her students; a closed mind catches only darkness.

Hoping to spark new memories, Olivia returned to the last place she saw David. After stilling her doubts, she rang the doorbell of the unremarkable house. It played a simple tune.

A young man opened the door. "Yeah?"

"I'm sorry to bother you, but my car's broken down. If it's not too much trouble, may I use your phone?"

The man shrugged. "Sure."

Olivia entered, surreptitiously scanning the interior. Nothing seemed out of place. There was certainly no captive psychologist anywhere.

"Phone's by the table."

"Thank you." She pretended to place a call. "David? Thank God I reached you. That car of mine has died again … I *did* have the mechanic check it. Will you come and pick me up? … One moment." Olivia turned to her host. "What street are we on?"

"Campbell Parade."

"It's Campbell Parade. Do you know it? … Okay. See you soon." She replaced the receiver before turning to her host. "I can't thank you enough for your kindness."

He shrugged. "It's cool."

"I've come from interstate to visit my son, David." Playing the dithering old woman, she withdrew a photo from her purse. "He's a good-looking boy, isn't he?"

The man studied the image. "He has your eyes."

Unless the man's acting skills exceeded Olivia's ability to read body language, he had never seen David before. The telltale signs of recognition were all absent.

The unremarkable house was apparently an unremarkable dead end.

***

A few days later Olivia arranged to meet Celeste at David's office. Apart from a small sign that read *Closed until further notice*, the place was just as she remembered.

"The police have already searched here." Celeste looked tired and fragile. "They didn't find anything."

Olivia rummaged through David's desk. "That doesn't mean there's nothing to be found."

"I've searched those drawers a dozen times myself."

"Did you find anything?"

"Only a headache."

Abandoning the desk, Olivia turned her attention to the office safe. "May I?"

Celeste entered the combination. "Go ahead."

Sifting through the safe's contents, careful not to let her enthusiasm show, Olivia quickly found what she was looking for. It was scrawled on a piece of soiled paper. "What happened to David's Escher picture?"

"Escher?" Celeste turned toward the pastel wall.

Olivia pocketed the invocation. "Did he remove it?"

"I think the frame got smashed." Celeste turned back to Olivia. "I'm not sure how."

"Perhaps I'll order David a replacement – as a gift for when he returns."

"*If* he returns." Celeste studied the city skyline, hugging herself as if cold. "We should have heard something by now. A call. A letter. A goddamn tweet."

Olivia stood beside Celeste, looking out at the view but not truly seeing it.

Silence consumed them both.

***

Armed with a mug of herbal tea, Olivia entered her study and retrieved a Latin dictionary from its wall of books. The heavy tome confirmed that *janua* was the Latin word for door. It was derived from Janus, an ancient Roman deity who presided over change, passage and transit. Olivia studied a drawing of the two-headed god. She went on to read that doors were considered to be semi-divine frames, marking the passage between danger and safety.

Sipping her tea, Olivia unfurled the slip of paper she had pocketed from David's safe. With the aid of the dictionary, she began translating the invocation. *Hic et illic, Januae, vos advoco.* Here and there, Doors, I summon you. *Magnae et parvae, Januae, vos saluto.* Big and small, Doors, I welcome you. *Intus et foras, Januae, vobis credo.* In and out, Doors, I trust you. *Nunc et tunc, Januae, vos honoro.* Now and then, Doors, I honor you. *His verbis et actis pactum consigno.* With these words and actions I seal the pact.

Once the translation was complete, Olivia reread the entire passage. Although she had hoped to find something extraordinary concealed within it, the translation proved underwhelming, like a butterfly without wings. Was this simple invocation truly a gateway into new realms of existence?

Regrettably, there was only one way to find out.

***

Lisa Cho took a sip of coffee. It was cold, having sat on her desk too long, so she spat it out. Unfortunately her case files were harder to expel. In particular, the file on David Druas was giving her a headache.

The psychologist had been missing for almost two weeks. Despite Lisa's best efforts – triangulating his phone, searching his apartment and office, checking his bank withdrawals and so on – she had been unable to find him.

His trail was as cold as the coffee in her cup.

THE RETURN

David's eyes snapped opened.

"I'm alive!" he marveled.

The maze, with its infinite dead ends, was gone. More astonishing, his emaciated body was now perfectly healthy, lying on the porch of a nondescript house. He began sobbing tears of joy.

A young man exited the house, wielding a baseball bat. "Another day, another druggie."

David staggered to his feet, stepping away from the newcomer. That was when he spotted the amber door. This place, he realized, was the spot he had brought Olivia to before losing himself in the maze.

The man lowered his bat. "You're the guy from the picture. I spoke to your mom."

"It's not me with the drug problem." David withdrew from the property, unable to wipe the smile from his face. It felt awesome to be alive.

***

After wandering aimlessly for several minutes, David entered the first convenience store he could find. Even though he wasn't hungry, he bought a protein bar, two bags of chips, a block of chocolate and a soda. With the memory of starvation still upon him, he stepped outside and gorged the lot.

Feeling slightly queasy, he hailed a cab. It smelled of cheap perfume, vinyl seats, and a stale lemon deodorizer. There were greasy finger marks on the window, and the floor was stained. Oddly, David felt nothing but gratitude. The shoddy cab, after all, was a welcome anchor to the world he knew.

When he finally entered the foyer of his apartment building, David's feeling of gratitude intensified. This was his home, his safe haven.

"Dr Druas!" The concierge gaped at him. "You're back."

"Glad to be home, Roger."

"You've had us worried."

David paused.

"Your secretary's been calling every day to ask if I've seen you. The police even came to search your apartment."

"You let the police into my home?"

"We thought something had happened to you." The concierge blushed. "We thought you were dead."

Hadn't he been? The truth made David shudder.

"Dr Druas, are you okay? You look a little pale."

"I'm fine, Roger. I'll be fine." David tried not to think of Hans Werner's warning – "*Not all injuries are physical*" – as he headed for the elevator.

When David entered his apartment, a new horror awaited him. The place was trashed. Someone had gone through every room, overturning furniture and spilling items onto the floor. His life literally lay in ruin.

***

"Your missing shrink just resurfaced," the desk sergeant advised Lisa. "He phoned in to report a break and enter."

Fifteen minutes later, Lisa was knocking on Apartment 608 of the swish building she had visited only days before. After a few moments, the door opened and a handsome face peered out at her.

"Dr Druas," she said. "I'm Officer Lisa Cho."

"Thanks for coming so promptly. Please, come in."

Lisa stepped into the apartment, which now resembled a trash heap. "You need a good cleaner and a good cop – not necessarily in that order."

"Are you good?"

"I guess we're about to find out."

***

David watched Lisa pace through his apartment, inspecting the discarded memorabilia of his life. She looked disconcertingly thorough.

"Do you know if anything's missing?"

David shrugged. "It's hard to say."

"This was no random break-in. Whoever did this was looking for something specific, or looking to send you a specific message. Someone you know, probably."

"I work with unbalanced people daily, but none of my clients would do this."

"Not *every* day."

"Excuse me?"

"You weren't at work this past fortnight. Why was that?"

The question made David uneasy. "With all due respect, Officer Cho, you're here to investigate a break-in. Not my travel schedule."

"The two could be related."

"I seriously doubt it."

"Police resources were used to search for you, Dr Druas. I think I deserve an explanation."

David smiled innocently. "Sometimes urban life can be overwhelming. I exchanged the bustle of the city for the greenery of nature."

"You didn't think to contact anyone?"

"There was no reception."

"Celeste Ellewood described you as Mr Responsible."

"It was never my intention to be gone so long. The truth, although embarrassing, is that I got lost. It's that simple."

"Life is rarely simple." Sounding skeptical, Lisa padded toward the main entry door. "This lock hasn't been forced. Does anyone else have a key?"

David thought about his plans to give Celeste a key, but those plans were long buried. "Only the concierge."

"I'll speak to him. I'll also get statements from your neighbors, and have an officer fingerprint your apartment."

An investigation sounded intrusive. "I'd prefer to close the door on this issue."

"You'll need a police report to make an insurance claim."

"There's nothing to claim because my possessions are all here." David forced another smile. "As you said, I just need a good cleaner."

FALLING

The night was black and frigid.

David floated in the blackness, perched on a spongy cloud. Below him, the city's massive towers resembled toy blocks. They were stacked in neat rows, divided by ribbon-like streets, and dusted with lights. It was a repetitive grid, populated by small people, in small houses, living small lives. Welcome to Lego Land.

Beside him, Avan sat on his own cloud, wearing a traditional Indian sherwani. "The world is like a painting. A painting with blocks and people and colorful things." His yellow sherwani turned blue.

"Blocks and people and colorful things," David agreed.

"The people made the blocks, but who do you suppose made the people?"

David studied Lego Land, before gazing toward the heavens. "Perhaps it was the same person who painted the stars onto the sky."

"A painter?" Avan sounded skeptical.

"An *artist*."

"Did this artist also create color?" Avan's sherwani turned orange. The transformation seemed utterly natural, like having philosophical discussions on clouds.

As David considered Avan's question, an answer flitted into his mind. "Color trolls created color! But trolls don't like black, which is why black isn't in rainbows. Black is shunned, like a leper eating licorice."

Avan reached into the folds of his sherwani and pulled out two licorice sticks. He bit into one and handed the other to David. "Did you always want to be a psychologist?"

David nodded. "I liked solving mysteries as a kid."

"What do mysteries have to do with psychology?"

"Are you kidding me?" David spoke between mouthfuls. "The biggest mystery of them all is the human mind. It doesn't get much bigger than that."

"When I was a child, I liked playing dress up. Acting was my escape." Avan's sherwani turned rainbow colored, as he sprang to his feet and twirled grandly. He finished with a practiced bow.

On the clouds above the world, David clapped. The moment was augmented by music, arising from an unknown source. Although he had never heard the song before, David had always known it. They sang together.

When the song was over, David studied Avan's beaming face. "You're cheerful tonight."

"I have a failsafe recipe for happiness."

"Care to share?"

Avan's sherwani sparkled green like a freshly watered lawn. "The secret to happiness can be summed up in four sentences: *Fly like a dragon; Burn like the sun; Shoot like a cannon; Fuck like a nun.*"

David laughed. "Do nuns fuck?"

Avan's green sherwani turned gray. "That's the whole point, silly: when something is prohibited, it makes us want it even more."

"Do you ever wish your life could be different?"

"I wish many things." Avan's sherwani turned as black as the night. Looking at him was like looking at a head with no body. It was disconcerting.

"What do you wish for?"

"Have you ever played *Guess the Object?*"

David shook his head.

"Give me your hand." Avan placed something in David's palm, closing his hand around it. "I wish you knew what you held."

The object felt small and cold. "Is it something important?" David asked.

"Not to you." Avan's sherwani turned an angry red. "Have a look."

David gingerly opened his hand, finding a gold heart that was cracked down the middle.

"Now you know." Stretching out his arms, reminiscent of an Indian Christ, Avan let himself fall.

"No!" David screamed.

Instead of flying like a dragon, Avan fell like a rock. As his body cut through the air, his eyes held David tighter than a hangman's noose. When he finally hit the ground, his red sherwani spread out in all directions, creating a pool of red guilt.

A thumping beat intruded upon the sickening image.

***

David awoke, drenched in sweat. Although minor details would change, the nightmare refused to abate, even after all these months.

A thumping beat reverberated through his apartment.

Hauling himself out of bed, David staggered through the mess that littered his home. When he opened his front door, he found himself staring at Lisa and her burly male colleague. Neither officer looked pleased.

THE INTERVIEW

David sat in the interview room, opposite Lisa Cho and Phil Hollingsworth. The officers hadn't given much away, other than stating they needed his *assistance* in an urgent matter. A video recorder filmed proceedings.

"Why am I here?" David asked.

Lisa consulted her notebook. "Around 2:00 am, police responded to an emergency call. When they got to the scene, they discovered the caller – a Mr Hans Werner – had been murdered. Did you know him?"

David gaped at the revelation. "He was one of my clients."

The officers exchanged a glance as if to say *bull's eye*.

"Is that why I'm here?" David speculated. "To provide a psychological profile?"

"Not exactly," Lisa said. "Where were you around 2:00 am, Dr Druas?"

"At home asleep. Why?"

"You didn't visit Mr Werner at that time?"

David shook his head.

"Then perhaps you can offer an alternate explanation for this emergency call." Lisa activated a hand-held voice recorder, placing it on the table between them.

"Police department," said a female voice.

"Please, help me!" Hans Werner's voice was unmistakable. "He's got a knife!"

"Who's got a knife, sir?"

"Dr Druas. He broke into my house, threatening to kill me. I've never seen him this angry before."

"Sir, I need your name and location."

"Hans Werner." He sounded terrified. "Sixteen Donwahler Crescent."

"Are you able to get somewhere safe?"

"I'm locked in my bedroom. He's banging on the door, trying to get in. I don't know what to do."

Lisa turned off the recorder.

David was stunned. "Hans must have been … confused."

"You don't think Mr Werner would be able to tell the difference between his psychologist and some random assailant?"

Before David could respond, the interview was interrupted by a knock at the door.

"Excuse me." Lisa stepped away briefly, before returning with a small metal box. After whispering something to Phil, she focused her attention on David. "Do you know what's in this box?"

"I'm not a mind reader, Officer Cho."

She opened the box, revealing a butcher's knife sealed in plastic. "This is the weapon that killed Hans Werner. Do you recognize it?"

David shook his head.

"Then how do you explain your fingerprints on it?"

"There must be some mistake."

"I personally attained your prints, when you were missing, via your safe deposit box. The match is conclusive."

David shivered as he studied the bloodied knife. "Someone must have stolen it from my kitchen. You know I was ransacked."

"I know you *claim* to have been."

"This is ridiculous. Can't you see I'm being framed?"

"By a person who looks like you?" Phil smirked.

Anger flared in David's chest. "Hans must have been coerced."

"Is that your story now?"

"It's *not* a story!" David thumped the table.

"That's quite a temper you have," Lisa goaded him. "It's easy to see why Mr Werner was so scared of you."

"I already told you, I wasn't there." David decided to qualify his statement. "Not recently."

"But you have visited him previously?"

David hesitated. "It was weeks ago."

"Do you visit all your clients, or just the ones that ignite your anger?"

Like a lamb tied to the spit, David realized there was no escaping the heat. "I want my lawyer." The smell of singed meat, he imagined, lingered in the air.

***

David's lawyer, Frank Stockton, arrived forty minutes later. His assessment of the situation was grim.

"It's stacked against you, David. I won't lie. It's stacked higher than the Himalayas."

"I'm innocent, Frank. You believe that, don't you?"

Frank placed his hand on David's shoulder. "How long have we known each other?"

"Twenty years?"

"Try twenty-five. That's a long time, long enough for me to know you don't have a murderous bone in your body." He paused. "Unfortunately, the jury won't just take my word for it."

"So where does that leave us?"

"Dangling on a mountain. We have to prove you were set up."

"How?"

"We'll argue the knife was planted. Only a fool would have left it behind, and we both know you're no fool." Frank paused, running a hand through his silvery hair. "The real problem, as I see it, is Werner's emergency call."

David nodded. "It sounded convincing."

"Himalayas."

Silence filled the claustrophobic consultation room.

"Can you get me bailed?"

"Not likely. They'll probably move you to the state penitentiary."

"I can't go there, Frank."

"I'm sorry, David. You don't have a choice."

"Can you at least arrange for me to have a psychological assessment?"

Frank frowned. "Why?"

"I want to buy some time." A plan was formulating

in David's head. "It needs to be an *external* assessment. I don't want one of their psychologists assessing me here."

"That might be harder to arrange."

"Have Olivia Milner help you. With all her connections, she'll know what strings to pull."

"I'll do my best." Frank eyed David uncertainly. "I just hope you know what you're doing – that mountain you're climbing has a steep drop."

CELESTE ELLEWOOD

Beautiful was the word most often used to describe Celeste. Despite such praise, she struggled to find love, often attracting men who were analogous to fish and chips. Greasy. Convenient. Bad for one's health.

True love seemed elusive, having struck only twice in her lifetime. The first, occurring at the supple age of nineteen, involved an older man who turned out to be married. In more recent years her attention shifted to an eligible bachelor, much closer to her own age.

Falling in love with David Druas was as easy as walking through fallen leaves, the kind that crunch pleasantly underfoot. Although he initially resisted the idea of an office romance, his aversion waned over time, like fallen leaves returning to the warmth of the earth.

Proceeding slowly, the pair eventually began dating. A romantic dinner. Movies followed by a moonlit stroll. The exchange of small gifts. It was the entrance into love's door. Unfortunately, as their romance was poised to enter a new and deeper phase, the dream morphed into a nightmare due to the actions of one man.

Avan Singh's unexpected death impacted like a frigid rain. The aftermath saw David withdraw into a shell, becoming depressed, sullen and consumed by remorse. Passion's fire had been extinguished by guilt's flood.

During those troubled days, Celeste did all she could to comfort the man she loved. Instead of accepting her efforts, however, David pushed her away. His words still echoed in her thoughts.

"To fraternize with clients or staff is to invite misery," David told her.

"What we have makes me more than *staff*," Celeste responded.

"You're drawing a salary. I'm paying you. You're staff."

The drop from courted woman to employee was embarrassingly painful. On several occasions Celeste offered to resign, wanting to give their budding relation-ship a chance to bloom. But it was to no avail.

"Avan Singh was not my client when he died," David insisted. "He was my *former* client, just as your resigna-tion would make you my *former* secretary. However you spin things, work-related ties are toxic."

From that time onward, Celeste's dreams began to wither. She continued working in the office because she enjoyed the role. Secretly, however, she hoped David would eventually change his mind. Cupid's arrow, once launched, was difficult to dislodge.

When David disappeared, after speaking to Hans Werner, Celeste feared the worst. Despite keeping in regular contact with the police and those connected with David, in her mind, the stench of foul play became stronger and more rancid with each passing day. David would never *purposely* disappear. She wept like a widow.

A few weeks after the disappearance, Olivia rang with some unexpected news. "David's been found."

"Thank God," Celeste exhaled. "Where was he?"

"Where he was seems less important than where he is." Olivia paused. "Celeste, David's been arrested for murder."

Although Celeste heard the information, it was difficult to process. David wasn't a murderer. He was a gentle man who would make a damn good husband. The carpet rose up to meet her. Or perhaps she slunk to the floor. "I don't understand."

"Nor do I," Olivia admitted. "Details are still sketchy but, according to David's lawyer, the victim's name is Hans Werner."

Of all the possible names in the world, that particular name was perhaps least surprising to Celeste. "David began acting weird since the day Mr Werner visited the office."

"What does *weird* look like?"

Celeste spoke of David staring at walls, canceling appointments and being distracted. Her revelation was met by silence. "Professor Milner? Do you know something?"

"I know that David isn't guilty of what they're claiming."

"That makes two of us." Maybe love was blind.

As soon as the conversation ended, Celeste made attempts to visit David in jail. Despite her best efforts, permission was flatly refused. She would have to wait until his transfer occurred, the staff told her. It was a crazy situation.

Celeste thoughts began swirling like a washing machine set to tumble dry.

Her life was again tumbling out of control.

THE HOSPITAL

Twenty-four hours after speaking to his lawyer, in the wake of legal and medical wrangling, David was granted permission to obtain an assessment from the Martyr Hospital's psych unit. Frank brought him a fresh set of clothes, restoring a sliver of dignity.

"All dressed up with nowhere to go." Lisa cuffed David's wrists for the journey.

"The Martyr Hospital is somewhere. It beats a cell."

"If you're hoping an insanity plea will buy you a *get out of jail* card, think again." Lisa scowled. "This isn't Monopoly."

"I don't play games."

"That makes two of us." Lisa escorted David to the secure parking lot, where Phil had a car waiting for them. "Let's get this excursion underway."

On the way to the hospital David spotted several doors that were all tantalizingly out of reach. He kept silent until they reached their destination. "Assuming the presumption of innocence still stands, could you at least remove my cuffs?"

Phil laughed.

"The psych patients will get agitated if they see a handcuffed man," David persisted. "That's a guaranteed way to aggravate overworked staff, not to mention the assessors who have to submit a final report."

"For someone who doesn't play games, you maneuver well." Lisa removed the cuffs. "Just make sure you behave yourself, otherwise it will be game over."

Once they were inside the hospital, Phil approached the help desk for directions. Although David knew where the psych ward was located, he kept silent. There was no hurry, after all, because the evaluation itself was unimportant. The day's true objective was to find a door.

Despite the risks associated with using the doors, David believed they were his best chance of escape. Unfortunately, like a tree failing to yield fruit, the hospital was proving barren. Would it be better to pass or fail the psychological assessment? The question hadn't arisen before, because sitting *through* the test was never part of the plan.

When they eventually reached the psych ward, Olivia was there to greet them. She stood alongside the head of psychiatry, Dr Thomas Gray.

"The test will take about one hour to complete," Dr Gray told the officers. "I'll personally escort you to a viewing room where you will be able to watch the proceedings via closed-circuit TV."

Lisa shook her head. "We have to remain with the defendant at all times."

"Your presence in the assessment room will unduly influence the patient," Olivia said. "Any results will be invalid."

Lisa consulted with Phil, before offering a compromise. "I'll watch the test from your viewing room. Officer Hollingsworth will wait *outside* the actual test room. Is that acceptable?"

Olivia smiled. "Entirely."

Dr Gray escorted Lisa away, while the rest continued to the test room. As they neared their destination, a psych patient stepped toward the trio. After briefly making eye contact with Olivia, he brandished a gun.

"Fight injustice!" The patient placed the gun to his temple. "Fight the new order!"

Phil tackled the patient, knocking the gun from his hand. It fell to the floor with a soft clatter, the sound of plastic.

Olivia whispered two words. "Run. Up."

David capitalized on the diversion, dodging past stunned patients and healthcare workers. They stared at him with confused faces, as if unable to decide what the emergency was. Of course, Phil's pursuit may have helped them to speculate.

"Druas is doing a runner, Cho," Phil hissed into his radio. "Get over here!"

Following Olivia's advice, David ducked into a stairwell and ran *up* rather than down. He emerged onto a floor that was closed to the public due to renovations. Hope surged like a burst water main. Not only did this floor offer numerous places to hide, it contained a turquoise door.

As David hastened toward his goal, something crashed into his legs.

"The guilty always run." Phil had David pinned to the floor. He slapped on a pair of handcuffs. "But justice always wins out in the end. Now get the fuck up!"

David was wrenched to his feet.

Phil activated his radio. "Druas is in custody."

"Where are you?" Lisa asked.

"Sixth floor. Comin' down."

David was taken back to the stairwell and shoved inside. When Phil followed seconds later, a fire extinguisher smacked against his head.

"What are you doing?" David asked the person concealed behind the stairwell door.

Olivia checked that Phil was breathing, before using his keys to remove David's handcuffs. "You mean, aside from aiding and abetting an accused murderer?"

"I'm innocent."

"I wouldn't be helping you escape if you weren't."

David took Olivia's hands into his own. "I'm eternally grateful for what you've done, but I can't let you implicate yourself any further."

"David—"

"I need you to trust me, Olivia. Can you do that?"

"Of course." She spoke without hesitation.

"Then go. With a million thanks."

Olivia gave him an envelope filled with cash, and a warm embrace, before departing down the stairwell.

David returned to the turquoise door. He opened it eagerly, only to be confronted by an arctic landscape. The world looked cold and inhospitable.

"Put your hands in the air!" Lisa approached from a side hallway. She held a gun. "Now!"

David did as he was told.

"Where's Officer Hollingsworth?"

David pointed to the end of the corridor, where Phil could be seen emerging from the stairwell. He held a hand to his head as he staggered toward the pair.

Lisa reached for her handcuffs. "I warned you to behave."

David lunged for the turquoise door, bracing against an arctic chill, praying he wouldn't get a bullet in his back.

***

Lisa's gun was aimed at David Druas when he stepped toward the hospital wall and … Lisa vividly remembered being rushed to hospital, when she was six-years-old, after breaking her leg. As a child, she was always climbing trees.

"Cho? Why is your weapon drawn?" Phil asked.

Lisa was surprised to find her gun in her hand. "I … I'm not sure."

"Maybe the wall committed a felony," he joked.

Holstering her gun, Lisa noticed Phil was cradling his head. "You're bleeding."

"I think I took a knock."

Is that why we're at the hospital? It was difficult to think clearly. "We should find you a doctor."

"Do we have time?"

"There's always time for pills, poking and prodding."

They sauntered off, lost to their individual thoughts.

LOST

David studied the blank expression on Lisa's face, watching her through the turquoise doorway. She seemed surprisingly calm, as if it were an everyday occurrence for people to vanish into nothingness. When Phil joined her, they exchanged a few words before stepping away without a backward glance.

Strange and stranger, David thought.

His current environment was also a little strange. Despite looking like an arctic realm from Earth, the "snow" turned out to be dry, like sand, though its white particles were clumped together like ice. As for the sky, it was a soft pink, lit by a small reddish sun. The temperature was pleasantly mild.

Sitting down on the icesand, David gazed toward the turquoise door, which was embedded in the side of a small hill. He watched and waited.

***

Despite a long queue in emergency, it didn't take Lisa long to find a doctor for Phil. With the exception of life-threatening cases, doctors tended to put officers ahead of civilians as a mark of respect.

Ignoring the resentful glares of nearby patients, Lisa flicked through a glossy magazine. The publication, un-surprisingly, was focused on celebrities. It was frivolous and several months out of date, but it passed the time.

"Officer Cho?"

Lisa glanced up from the magazine to see a bearded man standing over her. Although she couldn't immedi-ately place him, his face was familiar. "Yes?"

"Did you find him?"

"I'm sorry, who?"

"Dr Druas. His assessment was supposed to begin half an hour ago."

Lisa flinched as slumbering memories awoke, dis-persing the fog of confusion. She recalled rushing to the sixth floor, after learning of David's escape, and finding him staring at a blank wall. But then what? That moment, that *crucial* moment, was missing.

Ignoring the dread churning in her stomach, Lisa turned to the man standing beside her, Dr Thomas Gray. "Where can I find hospital security?"

***

A hospital search, David suspected, could last a few hours. It would then presumably branch out beyond the hospital's walls. For these reasons he decided it would be best to remain off-planet for the entire day.

While contemplating his options, David was jolted as Lisa Cho stepped into view, lingering beyond the rectangular portal. She looked both quizzical and agitated, throwing glances up and down the corridor where she stood.

Although some people viewed psychologists as mind readers, they were limited to physical and verbal cues, just like everyone else. Right now David wished that wasn't so. He would have given a great deal to know what she was thinking.

A loud shriek shattered the silence. Glancing up, David spotted a large bird gliding across the pink sky. Roughly ten feet long, not including its tail, the creature resembled a phoenix. It was white, like the ground, and chilling to behold.

With scant groundcover available, David pressed himself against the base of the hill and crouched low. The creature circled the area a few times, then flew away. He waited until it became a speck on the horizon before turning his attention back to the doorway. Lisa had gone, but now he could see security guards and police officers occasionally walking past.

The search had begun.

***

Although the Police Captain was a small man, even by Asian standards, he had an imposing presence. Summoned to his office, Lisa resisted the urge to wipe her sweaty palms against her uniform.

"Where are we with the search?" he asked.

"A sweep of the hospital didn't find anything, so we're focusing on the surrounding area. All available units are on it." Lisa cringed, unable to hide her embarrassment.

The Captain scowled. "Your record, up until now, has been spotless." Lisa's photo and stats were visible on an electronic tablet on the desk between them. "But you got sloppy today. And I don't like sloppy."

For the first time in her professional career, Lisa had lied to her colleagues. According to her account, she took Phil for medical treatment, believing that David was simultaneously undergoing his scheduled assessment, having been apprehended. Since Phil was in a worse mental state than she was, no one could challenge the claim. They consumed it like stale bread.

"I'm sorry, captain." Lisa tensed her body in an effort to stop it shaking. "I swear I'll do everything I can to make it up to you."

"The only reason I'm not suspending you is because you know more about Druas than any of my other staff. Now get out there and find him!"

When Lisa exited the Captain's office, she rubbed her sweaty palms against her uniform. If only embarrassment could be rubbed away as easily. She needed to find David quickly to redeem herself. The Captain was, after all, her favorite uncle.

FOUND

Hours passed, during which time David spotted several more of the flying creatures. None spotted him, as far as he could tell.

The hospital corridor, visible through the doorway, had remained empty for some time now. That didn't mean the police were no longer searching for him; it simply meant the search had moved elsewhere.

To stave off boredom, David tried juggling some icesand. He was starting to get the hang of it when the man in the brown suit wafted past the portal. He glanced directly at David and smiled.

Was it possible? David inched closer to the doorway, but the man withdrew from view. David maintained a vigil, as if expecting the stranger to return.

"Are you looking for me?"

David turned to find the man in the brown suit behind him. "How did you …?"

"Arrive here?"

David nodded.

"I am a Doorkeeper, David. I speak the language of doors."

The familiarity grated. "How do you know my name?"

"It's my job to know. In many ways you are like a child who has discovered a loaded gun. Think of me as your watchful guardian angel."

David scoffed. "A responsible guardian would remove a gun from a child."

"Doors, once invoked, cannot be removed." He paused. "Only endured."

"That's comforting."

Ignoring the sarcasm, the Doorkeeper scanned the environment. "This world looks innocent enough, but you can't hide here forever."

"I don't need forever."

"Just long enough to sort out your problems, perhaps?" The Doorkeeper hesitated. "Forgive my rudeness, but why did you murder Hans Werner?"

"I didn't murder anyone!"

"Is that what you believe?" Pity filled his eyes. "Door travelers often become unhinged, acting out of character, and suppressing all knowledge of their wicked deeds. A dark spiral knows no end."

"I could never commit, let alone forget, a murder."

"Values tend to change after—" The Doorkeeper cocked his head to the side.

"What is it?"

"Company."

David thought the Doorkeeper was mistaken, until noticing three puma-like creatures stalking toward them.

Like the phoenixes, they were white, effortlessly blending into the environment. Two of the beasts had serrated horns on their heads. The third, possibly a female, had tiny spikes around her head and upper back. They all had razor-sharp claws.

If the Doorkeeper was afraid, it didn't show. Stepping away from David, he casually reached for a foot-long rod that hung from his belt. "It's always stimulating to meet the locals." The rod expanded into a yard-long staff.

When the first creature struck, the Doorkeeper lashed out with his staff. Although the weapon resembled an ordinary length of wood, it cut like a laser, slicing the animal in half. The wounds instantly cauterized.

The two remaining beasts roared in outrage. They separated, stalking the Doorkeeper from different directions.

"The natives aren't happy." A freestanding hematite door appeared beside the Doorkeeper. "Maybe you'll have better luck dealing with them."

When he disappeared through his summoned door, the snarling beasts shifted their focus to David. With few other options, he lunged toward his own portal as the female creature pounced.

Searing pain briefly cut across David's back, as claws met flesh. But then he was back in the hospital corridor, completely unharmed. He looked both ways before running to the elevator, which took him directly to the ground floor. No one tried to stop him as he hurried across the foyer, toward the main exit.

Once outside, he strolled off in a northbound direction, trying to act like any other departing visitor. When he spotted a cop car cruising toward him, David discarded the visitor act and ran.

***

Lisa studied a map of the city. She sat in the passenger seat of a patrol car, while her new partner, a rookie named Stanley Becroft, sped through the streets.

"Move out of the way!" he shouted, honking at some slow-moving pedestrians.

Being paired with a rookie during the middle of an active case was an unmistakable slight. Pushing her anger aside, Lisa pointed to a green area on the map, located northeast of the hospital. "There! That's where he's heading."

"The city park?" Stanley sounded skeptical. "I thought Druas was last seen traveling north*west* of the hospital?"

"People under pressure gravitate to the familiar. He used to jog through the park every morning." Her missing-person inquiry into David wasn't an entire waste.

"It's a long shot."

"No, it's a *hunch*, and you're going to follow it!"

Once they reached the park, Lisa opted to stand by the central fountain. Aside from the fact that multiple paths converged there, it was high ground with a 360° view of the entire area.

"Do you think Druas is guilty?" Stanley asked. "Of murder?"

"I think you should concentrate less on talking and more on watching."

As the minutes passed, Lisa began to regret her choice of locations. The park was full of joggers, students, and families. But there were no escaped fugitives. Her eyes swept over a couple pushing a pram. The father, wearing a baseball cap, lifted his head just long enough to meet her gaze. An instant was all it took.

"It's him!" she yelled. "It's Druas!"

At the sound of his name, David fled down the path from which he had come, ignoring the abuse shouted by his female companion. As Lisa gave pursuit, with a disbelieving Stanley at her heels, she activated her radio: "David Druas is in the city park. I need all available units to attend!"

Startled park goers gaped at the trio, as they cut through the otherwise serene environment, running at full pelt. Stanley routinely yelled for David to stop. His other catchcry was for pedestrians to move out of the way. Lisa chose to remain silent, concentrating on narrowing the gap. The hunters and the hunted all knew what was at stake.

David abruptly turned off the path he was on and began racing toward a brick toilet block. As he rounded the rear wall, hastening toward the facade, he was briefly lost from sight.

Stanley peeled off, circling around the other side of the toilet block, as Lisa followed hard on David's heels. The two officers met up around the front, but there was no sign of their quarry.

"He's making this too easy." Lisa drew her gun and entered the female toilets. They were empty, aside from a shocked teenage girl. When Lisa stepped back outside, she found Stanley simultaneously exiting the gents.

"He wasn't in there."

"Not again," Lisa said. "Is this guy Harry-fucking-Houdini?"

Stanley shrugged. "Either that or we've been chasing a ghost."

Despite the sunshine streaming through the trees, she was suddenly gripped by a cold dread.

***

Stepping through the toilet block's misshapen metal door, David emerged onto a rocky plain. Devoid of any greenery, the cracked ground was pebbled with massive boulders. They looked like marbles discarded by a careless giant. A mountain range loomed nearby, adding to the sense of desolation.

Ignoring the dry wind that stung his skin, David focused on the metal doorway. He could see Lisa standing with her lanky male partner. This time, however, she looked frustrated rather than relaxed. As David tried to fathom what they were saying, a hand clamped onto his shoulder.

"Jesus!" David recoiled in shock.

"Don't be scared, David," a familiar voice said. "I've come to help you."

David's shock increased exponentially as he peered into the eyes of Avan Singh.

BEAUTY (PAST)

The office clock showed 6:50 pm. David continued flicking through the textbook he was reading, but it was difficult to concentrate on facts and figures. Avan Singh was due at any moment.

Abandoning the textbook, David gazed out across the city. He recalled the night he and Avan had dinner together, the night they shared a kiss, several weeks ago. Since then, they had successfully avoided each other, but yesterday Avan broke the standoff, phoning him with an unusual request.

A buzzer pierced the silence.

David proceeded to the reception area and unlocked the main door.

"Avan, how are you?"

"Functional." He held a small urn.

"Are you ready to do this?"

Avan nodded.

David locked his office and escorted Avan to the

elevator. "First we have to pick up the key from the building manager. He's expecting us."

After visiting the building manager, they took the elevator to the highest floor. On that floor was a locked door marked: *STRICTLY NO ENTRY. THIS DOOR IS ALARMED.*

"Can all tenants access the roof?" Avan asked.

"Not usually. It's an insurance nightmare."

"You were given a key."

"The building manager's a personal friend of mine." David unlocked the door. "I helped his daughter overcome a problem."

Climbing a small stairwell, David led Avan out onto the roof. The city sparkled all around them, like a forest of Christmas trees. It was a stunning location, softly lit by the crescent moon that loomed overhead.

"This is perfect." Avan spotted the rooftop's only bench. "Could we sit for awhile?"

"Of course."

"Do you come here much?" Avan asked.

"This is my third time. I've never been up here at night." David watched a plane traverse the sky. He wondered where the passengers were headed. "How's Robin Hood shaping up?"

Avan shrugged. "I got booted from the cast."

"Why?" David tried to hide the shock in his voice.

"I missed too many rehearsals." Avan sneered. "Apparently actors aren't allowed to have personal problems."

"You should lodge a complaint."

"Since I couldn't pay my rent, I also got booted from

my flat. I guess that makes me the Sheriff of Nothing-ham."

"There are treatments for depression, anxiety. I can refer you to someone."

Avan smiled. It was a smile that said, *fuck you and your referral*. "I'm going away soon."

"You are? Where?"

"I don't know the itinerary." Avan's smile faded.

"Traveling can be healing. Refreshing. I see it in my clients all the time."

Avan lifted his urn. "I think it's time."

Abandoning the bench, they ambled toward the build-ing's edge.

"Every bird should ride the wind, both in life and death." Avan emptied the urn's ashes onto the breeze. "Goodbye William Shakespeare."

They stood in silence.

Under the moon. On top of the world.

The urn dropped from Avan's grip, rolling across the rooftop tiles.

David bent to retrieve it.

"So much beauty."

David froze. "Avan, come down from there!"

Avan paced along the ledge. "And forfeit the view? I don't think so."

"I don't want you to hurt yourself. Please, come down."

"Wanting and wishing are wasted pastimes. *You* taught me that."

"I know you're going through a rough time—"

"You don't know enough." Avan's voice was raw.

"I know the pain of loss. It stabs at my heart every time my mother fails to recognize me. I also know that help is available." David reached toward him. "Take my hand."

"I've already made my decision."

"Then I'm asking you to unmake it." David's voice trembled. "Avan, if you care about me, please don't put me through this."

"This isn't about revenge or hurting you. That's not why I'm here."

"Then why are you doing this?"

"If I'm going to leave this world, this little life, I want the last thing I see to be a thing of beauty – and I'm not talking about the city. You, David Anthony Druas, are all the beauty I need." Avan held David's gaze for an eternal moment, a moment without a beginning and without an end. He then jumped, plummeting to the ground.

"NO!" Insane with grief, David punched the ledge until his fist was bloody and raw. When he couldn't punch anymore, he fell to his knees and emptied his stomach. In that moment there was no beauty.

Beauty was an ugly lie.

AFTERLIFE

Standing on that rocky plain, David flinched at seeing his former client. The encounter was surreal, causing an avalanche of disbelief.

"We can't stay here." Avan glanced around nervously. "It's far too dangerous. You need to come with me."

David didn't move. "How is it you're here? How is it you're … alive?"

"We don't have time for this. I need you to trust me. Can you do that?"

When David nodded, Avan took his hand, guiding him away from the misshapen door. Together they traversed the arid ground, weaving past discarded boulders as they hastened toward the nearby mountain range. The wind continued to howl.

After a time David pulled to a halt, needing to catch his breath. "I'm not going any further. Not until you tell me what's going on."

Avan hesitated. "This is *their* territory. If they catch you, they will acquire your soul."

"Who are *they*?"

"The demons." Avan sounded afraid. "I know a safe place not far from here."

They followed a concealed mountain path that led to a tunnel.

"In there?"

"It's safe. You need to trust me, David."

The tunnel's interior passageway was perfectly straight and lit by flaming torches. After following it for several minutes, David spotted a glowing archway in the distance ahead. "What's that?"

"It's the safe place I told you about." Avan's face was lit by joy and the torch's flickering light. "The other side of the mountain."

"Already?" David frowned. "How could we have cut through the mountain this quickly?"

"In the oasis, all things are possible. Come."

When they emerged on the other side of the mountain, a lush oasis spread out before them. It was the complete opposite of the landscape they had just fled.

"This way." Avan descended the mountain.

The oasis, it turned out, was teeming with life. Not only were there exotic birds, lizards, and mammals, there were also people. Although some looked like they were plucked directly from Earth, others looked slightly off. For example, there was a man with elfin ears, a woman with purple skin, and a child covered in fur. None of the inhabitants acknowledged David's presence.

"Who are these people?"

"Ignore them," Avan cautioned. "Provided we leave them alone, they won't trouble us." He led David deeper into the oasis, drawing him toward some unseen goal. "Are you thirsty?"

"A little," David admitted.

"Let's take a break." They sat on a patch of lush grass. Avan handed David a flute of sparkling wine. "Drink."

David started. "Where did you get that?"

"The oasis provides for its inhabitants." Avan smiled. "Drink."

David drank the wine. It tasted delicious, soothing his troubled mind.

***

After a little more trekking, David and Avan reached a log cabin.

"Welcome to my home."

The cabin's exterior reminded David of a holiday house his parents once rented for the summer. Inside, however, it was like an Aladdin's cave. Not only did ornate furniture fill each room, exotic collectables lay everywhere, often studded with rare gems.

"What do you think?"

"It's spectacular." David stroked a gold bust of Ganesha.

"I'm glad you like it, because now it's your home too."

"I can't stay here, Avan."

Avan stepped toward a covered platter that sat on the dining table. "You must be hungry after traveling. Do you still like seafood?" He lifted the lid, revealing a seafood feast. Its pungent aroma infused the air.

"I'm not hungry."

Avan replaced the lid. "Would you prefer steak?" He lifted it again, this time revealing a medium-rare porterhouse steak, steaming potatoes and Brussels sprouts, all drenched in gravy.

"Is this heaven?" David recalled the rocky plain. "Or hell?"

"The oasis is whatever you make it."

"I don't belong here, Avan. I'm not dead."

For a fleeting moment, everything within the cabin withered, before returning to its original splendor. Avan didn't seem to notice. "I want you to stay."

***

"You're going to like it here, David." Avan padded through the lush flora. "This place grows on you."

The statement left David feeling troubled. It was a subtle discomfort, like a few grains of sand lingering in a new pair of shoes. He decided to change the subject. "Who were the people we saw earlier? Are they dead?"

Avan rounded on him. "They're no one! You need to forget about them."

"Can you at least tell me why?"

"The inhabitants value their privacy. You should avoid seeking them out until you're one of us. That's not too much to ask, is it?"

"No," David lied.

"Good." The smile returned. "Do you still like to swim?"

They came to a secluded spring, nestled underneath a waterfall that fell like a shower of diamonds from the emerald cliffs above. Exotic flowers grew abundantly at the water's edge, adding to the beauty.

Avan began removing his clothes. "What are you waiting for?"

"I don't have any bathers."

"You don't need any here." Avan was comfortable with nudity.

David shook his head. "I don't think so."

"If you want bathers, declare it to be so. The oasis always provides."

David unbuckled his pants, surprised to be wearing a pair of Speedos. They raced to the spring like a couple of kids. It was easy to feel young in a place where wishes blossomed. The water was a perfect temperature.

"A person could get used to living like this." David spotted movement behind a cluster of ferns. The purple woman, the one he had seen on his arrival, quickly ducked out of view.

Avan, unaware of the intrusion, paddled closer to David. "Does that mean you'll stay?"

All that awaited him on Earth was some blinkered cops, a murder trial, and a stalled career. David had to admit he was tempted. "For awhile."

Avan congratulated him with a hug. "You'll be happy here."

The gesture made David uncomfortable. He gently extricated himself from the embrace. "We've been over this ground before."

Avan glowered. "Have it your way."

The still water began to churn rapidly, as if stirred by an unseen hand. Trapped in the center of the violent whirlpool, David wondered if it was possible to die while visiting the afterlife. As the current dragged him under, twisting his body like a puppet, he feared he would soon find out.

LISA CHO

The Captain was scanning budget reports when his secretary's voice came over the intercom.

"Officer Cho has just arrived. Should I have her wait?"

Given Lisa's recent incompetence, the Captain was tempted to have his niece wait in a cell. Instead, he pressed the intercom button and said, "Send her in."

After a moment, the door opened and Lisa entered. Her face was set in a grimace, as though she had bitten into something rancid. "You wanted to see me, sir?"

"Office chairs aren't made for admiration." As Lisa seated herself, he continued scanning the budget reports. After signing off on one of the recommendations, and striking through another, he finally put the documents aside. "How is your memory, Officer Cho?"

She shook her head. "Sir?"

"You remember what I said about *sloppy*?"

Lisa hesitated. "You don't like sloppy."

"I despise it," the Captain insisted.

"Losing David Druas was not due to ineptitude."

"Then what the hell was it due to?"

Lisa bit her lower lip. "I don't know how to answer that question, sir, because in all honesty I don't know how he managed to get away."

"*Don't know* is an aphorism for sloppy. It's the reason you're being relieved from field duties."

"Relieved?" Lisa looked taken aback, like a bird clipped of its wings. "For how long?"

"Indefinitely!" Flight, the Captain knew, was a privilege.

"But uncle—"

The Captain motioned for silence. "If not for your clean record, we'd be discussing suspension. Now, unless you want to anger me further, I suggest you report to the Duty Officer to get your new caseload." He reached for the budget reports. "Please close the door on your way out."

***

Relieved from field duties. The words echoed in Lisa's head as she stormed out of the Captain's office.

The whole point of joining the police force, as she saw it, was to experience the excitement of fieldwork. Whether returning a stolen wedding ring to a widow, seizing heroin destined for the streets, or reuniting worried parents with their lost child, every second held the potential to make a positive difference. But you couldn't do that from behind a desk.

"Fuck you, David Druas."

The words jolted a nearby cleaner. Lisa ignored the elderly worker as she passed him by, calculating her next step. Although the Duty Officer would be expecting her, there was time to make a small detour.

Entering an unused room, Lisa logged onto a computer terminal and pulled up all the available files on David Druas. Although it was tedious work, she reread every scrap of information, hoping to find some new clue to the fugitive's current whereabouts.

After sifting through everything, Lisa was forced to admit defeat, frustrated by yet another failure. She was about to log off when she spotted an audio file labeled: *911-Werner.* When she listened to the recording, using a set of high-quality headphones, it almost felt as if she were in the room with the deceased.

Lisa gasped as something occurred to her.

Despite Werner's claim – *"I'm locked in my bedroom. He's banging on the door, trying to get in"* – Lisa couldn't hear any banging whatsoever. No matter what settings she chose, there was only background silence. Although it could have been a defect of the phone, something about this call suddenly seemed very wrong.

She needed to speak to a sound technician.

DECEPTION

David lost consciousness as he sank beneath the swirling water. When he came to sometime later, he was lying in a comfortable bed. The log cabin held him like a wooden cocoon.

"We almost lost you." Avan offered a reassuring smile.

David feigned gratitude. "Thanks for rescuing me."

"I guess this kind of makes us even."

"Even?"

"I don't blame you for my death, David."

"Avan, I—"

"You did everything you could to save me. I saw it in your eyes as I slipped from your grasp."

"That's not what happened." Since Avan's death, all those months ago, David often replayed the events in his mind. Rather than remembering what had actually happened, he would imagine grasping Avan's hand, trying to pull him to safety. The lie softened his pain. "I never reached you."

Avan glowered as if tricked. "Let's not talk about the past. Not when we have the future of our choosing ahead of us."

A troubling suspicion brushed David's mind, as he gingerly got out of bed.

"Does your body feel okay?" Avan fussed.

"Never better." David glanced out of the window, noticing twilight had descended. He would have to delay his departure until the morning. "What do you do here? To pass the time?"

"You name it. The oasis always provides."

David decided to make the most of his temporary captivity. The right questions, after all, could prove useful. "How exactly does manifestation occur?"

"It's all about intention. You simply have to believe."

"That's it?"

Avan nodded.

David held out his hand, believing he was holding a globe of the Earth. Sure enough, one instantly appeared in his palm. The tiny blue and green sphere almost caused him to weep. "Are these creations real?"

"You tell me. Does it feel real?"

"Objects feel real in a dream." David allowed the globe to dissipate. "But when we wake from the dream, we realize the objects were illusory."

"This is no dream, David. It's paradise."

***

It seemed that paradise was good for one thing – indulgence. During the course of the night, they enjoyed food, wine and music that were unsurpassed. They played chess with diamond pieces, and Monopoly with real money. David even took a bath in liquid gold. Oddly, these extravagant actions left him feeling unfulfilled.

At the end of it all he retired to his bed, a canopied monstrosity dripping in silk sheets, and contemplated his escape. Would the door be easy to find? If he got lost, he figured he could always conjure up a map.

As he began to drift off to sleep, lulled by the vintage alcohol in his system, the bedroom door creaked open. The intrusion annoyed him. "What do you want, Avan?"

Celeste glided forward, wearing a sheer nightgown. "You mistake me."

David scoffed. "I never summoned Celeste."

"Are you sure about that?" Celeste discarded her nightgown, revealing full breasts and a shaved pubic area.

"What are you doing?" David got an erection as she slid into the bed.

"Don't fear pleasure, David." Celeste placed his hand between her legs. "What is paradise, if not an opportunity to indulge ourselves?"

David hesitantly kissed her lips. They tasted like cherries. Her skin was as smooth as the silky sheets on which they lay. When he moved to penetrate her, she molded to his body. David found himself slipping into an ecstasy that was raw, passionate and unbridled. He gave himself to the moment.

Their lovemaking was ecstatic, until David peered into the eyes of the woman who lay beneath him. Instead of seeing Celeste, he glimpsed a gnarled creature that resembled the stuff of nightmares. The sight made him recoil in horror.

"What's wrong?" The creature once again wore Celeste's face and body.

David willed a baseball bat into his hand and cracked it over her head. As he fled the cabin, entering the starlit oasis, he summoned shoes and clothes. Unfortunately no amount of intending could scrub away the disgust from his skin.

"You can't run, David." Avan staggered onto the cabin's porch, clutching his head. "You're mine now. I'll always find you."

Turning on his heels, David fled through the trees toward the mountains.

***

After running for the better part of an hour, David took shelter behind some trees, still haunted by the deception. Avan Singh was dead, he reminded himself. *If* his soul existed, living eternally in some afterlife, it wasn't here.

He manifested a jug of water and drank greedily.

David lowered the jug as an idea dawned. "Manifestation!"

Focusing his thoughts, David willed the misshapen metal door *to* him. When it appeared, he quickly stepped through it, desperate to return home. Instead of reemerging onto Earth, however, he found himself still standing in the oasis. This particular door, like everything else, was a deceit.

A twig snapped nearby. David crept forward, wearing the shadows as he weaved through the trees. He found the purple woman standing in a clearing. Although her back was toward him, he felt certain she was aware of his presence. He willed a gun into his hand and stepped out from the tree line. "Who are you?"

"Today I am a purple lady." She turned around. "Tomorrow will be a new day."

"Do you have a name?"

"Names are meaningless for those lacking true faces." She studied David's gun. "Can you trust that weapon to fire bullets and not … flowers?"

Troubled by the question, David let the gun dissipate. He could always summon another baseball bat if needed. "Your physical form is an illusion?"

"Everything is an illusion."

"Everything within the oasis," David corrected her.

The woman remained silent.

"That was you at the spring, wasn't it?"

"Visitors rarely come to the oasis. I was curious to speak with you."

"Why didn't you?"

"By our law, you belong to the one who found you. It would have been improper for me to initiate contact."

"I don't belong to anyone! And I don't belong here."

"I have not come to stop you, but to wish you well, David Druas."

"How do you know my name?"

"Your surface thoughts, and those strengthened by deep emotion, are clear to us. Do not fear what awaits you on the other side of the mountain. There are no demons – at least not *outside* the oasis."

"Why are you telling me this?"

"Because not all beasts are bad." She retreated into the darkness of the night.

David called after the woman, but she neither responded nor returned. With few options available, he continued toward the mountain range, charting a haphazard course by the starlight. His thoughts were of a purple lady who helped ease the mind of a stranger – surely the act of an angel rather than a beast.

***

Hours later, David passed through the mountain's torchlit tunnel and stepped into the dry wind beyond.

As the purple lady had promised, no demons lay outside the oasis. There were no life-forms whatsoever. He followed the concealed path down the rocky mountain. At one point, when he glanced over his shoulder, he noticed Avan – or rather, the *thing* impersonating Avan – glaring at him from the tunnel's entrance. Whatever it was, it appeared unwilling or unable to follow. The con was over.

Relief surged through David when he finally reached the misshapen door. Unlike the previous construct, it was a genuine portal home, leading to the moonlit city park. He stepped through the metal frame, glad to be returning to Earth. Only then did his body feel clean.

THE CORPSE

The city park was mostly deserted. As David hastened along one of the many pathways, he spotted a few vagrants, but there were no cops. According to his watch, it was 4:48 am.

Abandoning the park, he ventured onto the city streets, avoiding the few people who were about. A nondescript alley contained an ivory-like door that was carved with geometric shapes. Despite having reservations about traveling, David needed to escape those hunting him. He also needed time to gather his thoughts.

The ivory door, once opened, revealed an ultramodern city. Defying the limitations of architecture, its reflective buildings were clustered in mind-boggling shapes, representing a vision of the future.

Surprisingly the city was dead still. Would the city's inhabitants be welcoming or hostile? Unable to see any life forms, David was reminded of the anorexic forest, and the *hidden* creatures that lived there. Deciding to take a gamble, he stepped forward, bracing for a new adventure.

The instant David entered the mirror-like city, toxic gas flooded his lungs. As he fell to his knees, spewing blood onto the street, pain ripped through his entire body. The nightmare intensified as blood began leaking from his ears and eyes, turning the reflective city dark red.

Death claimed him.

***

When David's eyes opened, he inhaled eagerly, like a man who had spent a year under water. The fresh air filling his lungs was a vast improvement to the poisonous gas.

Having been returned to Earth, he lay in front of the ivory door. As David hoisted himself upright, he glanced toward the futuristic world. Unlike before, there was now a pool of blood on the other side of the doorway. In the blood lay a corpse.

"No ..." The body looked *exactly* like David. "That's impossible."

"Few things are impossible." The Doorkeeper stepped out of the alley's shadows, glancing toward the portal. "Though it is rare for a door to exist among so many reflective surfaces – they interfere with the cloaking process."

"I wasn't referring to the location!" David pointed at the corpse. "Who is that?"

"It's you, of course."

"But I'm *here*, in the alley."

"Think of the doors as human-sized scanners, able to reconstruct whatever passes through them. This inbuilt safety mechanism ensures that all travelers are ultimately returned to their home planet, *unaltered*." He paused. "If death occurs while traveling, another body is simply generated to house the spirit."

"Simply?" David was aghast. "Are you saying I'm a clone?"

"Are you dissatisfied with your new body?"

"I'm chuffed." David kicked a nearby dumpster.

"Flesh and bones do not make the man."

David was in no mood for a philosophical discussion. "How do you keep finding me?"

"I can sense when a door opens." He closed the ivory door. "I've come to ask you to turn yourself in to the police."

David sneered. "I'll turn myself in when Santa Claus impregnates the Tooth Fairy."

"This is not a joke, David. My task, as a Doorkeeper, is to guard the secret of the doors. The moment you killed Hans Werner, becoming a fugitive from your own kind, you endangered that secret."

"I *won't* confess to something I didn't do!"

The Doorkeeper looked resigned. "I didn't want it to come to this."

"A stalemate?"

"An ultimatum."

THE DOORKEEPER

Despite recent advances in technology, Earth was a fledgling planet by cosmic standards. Its inhabitants rarely invoked doors because few even knew such portals existed. According to Doorkeeper records, the last known summoning occurred more than five decades ago, in a tiny village in West Africa. That particular breach was followed by half a century of calm, during which time knowledge of the doors faded. Of course, more recently, all that changed.

When the latest breach occurred several weeks ago, it sent tiny ripples through the space-time continuum. Doorkeeper Amand, the keeper assigned to Earth and her sister planets, immediately began searching for the source. That was a Doorkeeper's role: to monitor and minimize unauthorized usage.

The culprit proved to be a middle-aged accountant living an otherwise unremarkable life. Although invoking the doors was not a crime, the invocation itself could not be allowed to spread. There were simply too many dangers. For this reason, the Doorkeeper began monitoring Hans Werner.

Unfortunately, instead of being contained, the secret eventually spread. When Hans Werner died, the Doorkeeper believed David's arrest would bring the matter to a close. He never expected the psychologist would become a fugitive.

Given that fugitives tended to attract unwanted attention, the Doorkeeper sought David out, hoping to reason with him.

"I didn't want it to come to this," the Doorkeeper admitted.

"A stalemate?"

"An ultimatum. Unless you surrender yourself to the police, those closest to you will be relocated."

"Relocated?" David frowned.

"Transported elsewhere. I will see to it myself. Without invocations, they will be unable to return to Earth or stave off death. I'm sorry it's come to this."

"I'm sorry too." David lunged at the Doorkeeper.

Anticipating an attack, the Doorkeeper simply transported himself twenty feet away. "At sunrise I'll be at the easternmost pier with Celeste Ellewood, awaiting your response."

"You leave Celeste out of this!" David rushed the Doorkeeper again, but he was already gone.

***

Celeste was dreaming about nuns and cherry blossom trees when the phone woke her. She reached for the receiver. "Hello?"

"Celeste, it's David. Are you all right?"

"David?" She sat upright. "My god, do you know how worried I've been about you? What have you gotten yourself into?"

"There's no time to discuss that now. You're in danger."

"Danger?"

"You need to get out of there," he insisted. "Go to your sister's. Go anywhere. Just leave the house *now*."

"David, it's 5:30 in the morning …"

"Do you still love me?"

Her answer was bittersweet. "Every day."

"Then meet me now, outside our favorite restaurant. This call's probably being monitored, but you know the place. I promise I'll tell you everything."

"I'm on my way." Celeste hung up the phone. Dressing quickly, she snatched up her car keys and hurried out the front door.

A stranger, impeccably dressed in a brown suit, stood waiting for her on the doorstep. "Going somewhere, Celeste?"

***

After binding Celeste's mouth and wrists, the Doorkeeper tried phoning David back, but his cell was switched off, presumably to evade police detection. He decided a simple text would suffice: *Celeste is tied up … but our original meeting place still stands. TDK.*

When the morning sun began to rise, David made an appearance. He studied Celeste, bound in her orange dress, as he traversed the length of the pier. "Let her go, you bastard!"

"Be at ease, David. Your friend is uninjured."

Celeste tried to shout something, but the gag muffled her words.

"If you hurt her, I'll end you."

"Gallant words. But actions always outweigh threats."

A hematite door appeared behind Celeste, revealing a desert-like landscape. She, of course, was unaware of the portal.

"Don't," David pleaded. "I'll surrender to the police."

"I knew you could be a reasonable man, given the right motivation." The Doorkeeper grinned. "From this moment on, you will forgo using all doors—"

The Doorkeeper grunted as Celeste kneed him in the groin. When David delivered a follow-up strike, he found himself plummeting into the sea. The water was unexpectedly frigid.

Ignoring the pain in his groin, and the chill in his bones, the Doorkeeper summoned a door. It failed to appear. Taking a calming breath, he tried again. This time the door instantly materialized, seemingly unaffected by the heaving waves.

By now David and Celeste were halfway down the pier. Of course, distance didn't matter to someone capable of instantaneous transportation. He paddled through the hematite door, appearing *ahead* of his two escapees. "You can't run from a Doorkeeper."

"But we can fight." David threw a punch.

The Doorkeeper, still dripping of seawater, grabbed David's fist mid-swing. "All beings are *not* created equal." He squeezed, exerting enough pressure to force David to his knees. "Isn't that right, Ms Ellewood?"

Although Celeste's wrists were still tightly bound, her mouth gag had been removed. She spat on the Doorkeeper's face.

Flinging David aside, the enraged Doorkeeper telescoped his belt cylinder into a staff. Before he could strike at Celeste, however, David flung himself in front of her.

"Please," he begged. "Do what you want to me, but don't hurt Celeste."

The Doorkeeper grimaced, knowing the game had changed yet again. Protocol, unfortunately, was very clear. "Come with me, ask no questions, and I won't decapitate your friend." He gestured toward the hematite door. "After you."

David kissed Celeste on the cheek. "Don't be scared."

He stepped through the doorway.

THE OFFER

After traveling through the Doorkeeper's hematite door, David emerged into an empty room. Measuring roughly thirty by thirty feet, its walls were devoid of windows and doors. Its air tasted antiseptic.

"Please excuse the lack of décor." The Doorkeeper stepped through the hematite door, which promptly disappeared.

Despite being well lit, the room lacked conventional lighting. Instead, the walls and the ceiling glowed. When David tried to touch one of the luminous walls, it retreated from his grasp. "What?!"

The Doorkeeper laughed. "Welcome to the paradox cell – an impregnable chamber that warps time, matter and space."

"You're imprisoning me?"

"*Freeing* you would be more accurate." His face turned serious. "I'm offering you the opportunity to become a Doorkeeper."

David scoffed. "After bullying me and threatening my friends?"

"When you laid down your life on the pier, you crossed a threshold. You possess intelligence, drive, adaptability, vitality and *self-sacrifice* – the five fundamental qualities of a Doorkeeper. I am obligated to offer you the role."

"Obligated by whom?" David asked. "The people who created the doors?"

"No one knows who created the doors, because they are older than ancient. I take my instructions from the Council of Doorkeepers – a diverse group of custodians that seek to unravel the technology behind the doors."

"You keep mentioning technology, but the doors seem more like ... magic."

"The line between magic and science is sometimes thin."

"There was no science in the invocation I used."

"Countless invocations exist, each calibrated to the traveler's home planet. Most are crude tools, involving actions or words to induce a *specific* level of consciousness." He paused. "Whoever or whatever created the doors used advanced coding. This coding somehow responds to consciousness and intention, summoning the doors into existence."

David eyed the Doorkeeper. "Does coding technology exist on your home planet?"

"Doorkeepers have been unable to locate any species that possess such knowledge. My own people, a race genetically similar to humans, are no exception."

"Are there many species, many civilizations, out there?"

"The universe is littered with them. That is why we always need more Doorkeepers." He paused. "The position comes with many benefits – your intelligence, stamina, strength and senses will all be enhanced. You will find the Council is very generous, provided you don't fail them, of course."

"Fail them? In what way?"

"A Doorkeeper's sole responsibility is to protect the secret of the doors. Failure to do so will see a Doorkeeper removed from his or her role. Fortunately this rarely happens because we tend to be diligent in our duties – as your friend Hans Werner discovered."

David's breath caught in his throat. "What *really* happened to Hans?"

HANS WERNER (PAST)

Hans awoke suddenly. He had been dreaming about sailing a yacht over clear, pristine seas. The voyage had been utterly enjoyable until the yacht struck rocks and began to sink. Strangely, by that time, the yacht had morphed into a ship that resembled the Titanic. It seemed that nothing, not even colossal size, could protect against the inevitable.

The bedside clock displayed 2:08 am. Hans shifted in his bed, aware that many of the dream's details had already started to fade from his memory. Holding onto them was like trying to hold onto streaming water. As he drifted back to sleep, readying himself for another nocturnal adventure, a piercing yelp reverberated through the house.

Pulling himself out of bed, Hans padded downstairs. "Mitzy," he called. "Wo bist du?" The house was still, as if holding its breath. When Hans entered the living room, his own breath faltered. A silhouetted man stood near the window.

"Who's there?" Hans tried turning on the light switch, but it was dead.

"Don't be alarmed, Hans. Calm yourself."

Hans recognized the voice. "What are you doing here, Dr Druas?"

"I needed to talk to you. What I have to say couldn't wait until morning."

Hans stalked into the living room, furious at this intrusion. "Did you break the window to get in?"

"Don't concern yourself over small matters. Not when larger concerns are looming."

Hans stumbled over something strewn on the floor. Feeling his anger spike, he switched on a nearby lamp. The glow revealed Mitzy, the would-be stumbling block, lying dead on the floor. Her neck was twisted to an impossible angle.

Surprisingly, David Druas was nowhere to be seen. Instead, a man in a brown suit stood by the window. It was the same man who had been loitering in the neighborhood for the past month. "Who are you? What did you do to my Mitzy?!"

"I am a simple man." His voice sounded cool, taking on a generic tone. "Unlike the doors that I monitor."

Hans gaped. "You know about the doors?"

"As a Doorkeeper it is my duty to know." He stepped closer. "It is also my duty to address transgressions." A butcher's knife glinted in his gloved hand.

Hans fled through the darkened house, bounding up the stairs. Upon entering his bedroom, he locked the door behind him and switched on the light. For added measure, he barricaded the door with a nearby chest of drawers.

Just as he was starting to feel safe, something cold and sharp pressed against his neck.

"Tell me where it is," the Doorkeeper hissed.

"What …?"

The blade pressed closer to Hans's neck, drawing a trickle of blood. "The invocation."

"I don't have it." Hans trembled. "I gave it to Dr Druas."

"Involving your psychologist was your second mistake. Your first mistake was believing you were worthy of such a gift."

When the knife slid across his throat, Hans felt a cool, stinging sensation.

His vision darkened, and all sensations ceased.

***

Dropping the knife, the Doorkeeper let Hans Werner slump to the floor.

After returning the chest of drawers to its original position, he transported himself into the adjacent hallway and kicked in the bedroom door. Everything needed to look credible, supporting the lie. He used the landline to place a call.

"Police department," said a female voice.

"Please, help me!" The Doorkeeper impersonated Hans Werner's voice. "He's got a knife!"

THE CELL

David glowered at the Doorkeeper, disgusted by his callousness. "I could never barter my soul the way you have."

"Are you refusing to become a Doorkeeper?"

"I'm refusing to become a *killer.*"

"We can only kill in self-defense, or when an invocation has been willfully disseminated." The Doorkeeper studied the cell's luminous walls. "Of course, murder isn't my only recourse."

David tensed. "What do you mean?"

"Did you think I would return you to Earth after sharing so many secrets?" He grinned. "Sensory deprivation apparently unhinges the human mind. Tell me, doctor, how long would it take for someone to lose their sanity in a place like this?"

David remained silent.

"Time, like aging and decomposition, ceases within these walls. You will experience an eternity of deprivation, squeezed into a single Earth second." The Doorkeeper snapped his fingers. "At the end of it all, when you can't even remember your own name, I'll return you to Earth. Your body will be young, but your mind will be withered and decayed."

David lunged for the Doorkeeper only to be swatted aside. He slid toward a wall that he never reached.

"Don't you see that fighting is useless? You have nothing left to fight for, not even your precious Celeste."

David ignored the taste of blood in his mouth. "You promised not to—"

"Sever her delicate neck? I kept my word, David." The Doorkeeper paused. "But the sea makes promises to no man."

"No!" David charged forward.

Moving with otherworldly speed, the Doorkeeper sidestepped the attack, placing David in a chokehold. His arm was like a vise. "You can't avoid the inevitable."

Unconsciousness darkened the white cell.

***

The night was black and lonely. David drifted through the blackness, floating on a Persian rug. It was a minor variation to a familiar sequence. Avan Singh was due at any moment.

Before the dream could develop, David's eyes snapped open. As he hoisted himself off the cool, white floor, into a sitting position, he realized he had been undressed. He was as naked as the cell. But that was the least of his problems.

Was Celeste really dead? The question throbbed in his heart. He shook the thought away, needing to focus.

The cell's luminous walls were roughly twelve feet high, placing the ceiling out of reach. The floor was white and shiny, like marble. It was the only part of the room that didn't glow. Rising stiffly to his feet, David padded over to the nearest wall. It retreated from his outstretched hand.

"Not again." Undeterred, he ran toward it as fast as he could. All the while, the luminous wall remained just beyond his grasp. When he changed tack and lunged toward a corner, both walls retreated. It was insane.

"Is this a dream?" he called into the echoing silence.

The cell was now a cavernous space, spanning hundreds of feet from corner to corner. Although David had run flat out for several minutes, his breath wasn't labored, his pulse wasn't elevated, and his body wasn't sweating. Fatigue, it seemed, was a concept rather than a reality.

This place was entirely wrong.

***

Seconds turned into minutes. Minutes inched into hours. And hours blurred into days.

The mind-numbing cell acted like a stasis chamber, somehow maintaining a set point for David's physical body. It was like being a god – minus the devoted subjects – because hunger, thirst and tiredness ceased to exist.

His emotions, by contrast, were in a constant state of flux. Anger, loneliness, denial and guilt all jostled with each other. Having two deaths on his conscience was like lugging two rotting corpses. Unfortunately, the paradox cell provided endless time to contemplate his failings.

It was impossible to gauge time accurately because there were no points of reference. In a windowless room, day and night become irrelevant. What's more, denied of biological precursors, there were no food cycles or sleep cycles to measure. Each moment surreptitiously leached into the next, producing a stream of sameness. The well-lit room never changed.

Given his professional background, David knew some techniques to minimize the effects of sensory deprivation. They were little tricks like memory games, physical exercise, visualizations, meditation, body awareness, and sleep – even though he was *never* tired. These temporary tools, however, could not last the depth of eternity.

***

As a psychologist, David viewed mental illness as a sickness that needed to be managed. As a prisoner, his perspective changed. Mental illness became like a monster, a white beast that needed to be guarded against. It kept snapping at his heels.

"I am David Druas," he often yelled. "I am a psychologist, a son, a friend, a good person. I am deserving of freedom."

Freedom never came.

When David wasn't chasing the expanding walls, the cell would gradually decrease in size, returning to its original proportions. He spent hours contemplating this enigma, but he couldn't understand it any more than a fox could understand the inner workings of a coil-spring trap around its leg.

His jailer, unlike the cell, was comprehensible. *"If death occurs while traveling, another body is simply generated to house the spirit."* Was that why the Doorkeeper stole David's possessions? After all, clothing stuffed down a throat could easily choke a person, as could a belt. It was the only explanation that made sense.

Although David deplored suicide, it would presumably return him to Earth. Of course, in an empty cell there were no knives, no guns, no nooses, and no pills. With limited options, he tried to brain himself against the floor. The second before impact, however, it turned as soft as a pillow.

Following the failed attempt, his thoughts kept returning to the fox in its trap, until the answer finally dawned on him. He didn't need to gnaw off his own arm to free himself, he just needed to spill enough blood.

With his mind already frayed at the edges, David took a deep breath of antiseptic air, in preparation for what he was about to do. A vein pulsed in his upturned wrist.

He bared his teeth.

WATER

A salty breeze caressed David's skin. Was he dreaming? When he opened his eyes, the light that greeted him wasn't soft and diffuse. Rather, it was bright and natural, streaming down from the sun. A seagull flew by overhead.

Exhilarated to be home, he lifted his fully clothed body off the pier's weathered planks. While marveling at the ocean, a stark contrast to the drab cell, he noticed an orange shape bobbing in the water, some fifty feet away.

"Celeste?"

Despite a lengthy confinement, David recalled the Doorkeeper's words: *"an eternity of deprivation, squeezed into a single Earth second."* He dove off the pier, slicing into the icy water.

Arm over arm, David raced toward the woman he loved. Frustratingly, much like the cell walls, she kept drifting further from him. He redoubled his efforts, narrowing the gap to several feet, before she sank from sight.

Diving beneath the water, David spotted ruffles of orange sinking toward the ocean floor. Kicking frantically, he descended to her side. With a secure grip, David reversed directions, laboring toward the shimmering light above.

When they broke the surface, David realized Celeste's wrists were still bound. Ignoring his protesting muscles, he paddled back toward the pier, struggling to keep her head above water. After climbing the small ladder, he managed to pull Celeste up, relying on adrenaline and emotion to bolster his efforts.

Wasting no time, David began CPR. All the while, he kept hoping Celeste would open her sparkling eyes and start breathing. But her body remained cold and still.

Celeste Ellewood was dead.

Tears, salty like the sea, gushed from David's eyes. He sat with her corpse in silence. There were no words to express his pain.

***

It was raining by the time David reached Olivia's house. Hunched under the weight of his sodden clothes, he rang the doorbell and waited.

"David?" Olivia's eyes widened as she opened the door. "What happened to you?

He opened his mouth to answer, but didn't have the words.

Taking his hand, Olivia led him inside. "We should find you some warm clothes."

"I tried," David stammered. "I tried to save her."

"Save who?" Olivia asked.

"Celeste." David closed his eyes, giving into exhaustion. It was Celeste Ellewood, not Avan Singh, who filled his dreams.

***

David awoke the following morning to the smell of a fried breakfast. He had a quick shower, letting the water rejuvenate his battered body, before joining Olivia in the kitchen.

"Did you sleep well?" she asked.

"As well as could be expected. Celeste is dead, Olivia."

"I know. It made the morning news." Olivia held up a newspaper. "A witness described a man leaving the scene. Was it you?"

David tensed. "I didn't kill her."

Olivia set a plate of sausages and eggs onto the table, next to the cereal and toast. "I'm not in the habit of making breakfast for murderers."

David scanned the food. "I'm not hungry."

"You need to restore your energy." Retrieving a jug of refrigerated water, Olivia filled their glasses. "Besides, you can't let me eat alone."

As rain continued to lash the house, David told her everything that had happened to him. Confession was cleansing. Like the rain.

REVENGE

David spent several days convalescing at Olivia's house. Each day Olivia would go to work, maintaining the pretense of her normal routine. At night, she provided intensive counseling, though both knew psychology could only go so far.

The prospect of revenge also soothed some of the pain. But there was a stumbling block. Since the Doorkeeper was a visitor to Earth, like all door travelers, he was protected against physical harm. After all, how do you kill someone who can be cloned in an instant?

It took hours of contemplation, but David eventually formulated a strategy. After sharing his plan with Olivia to help smooth out the details, he borrowed her car to visit one of his clients.

Eugene Taylor was a computer programmer and internet hacker who suffered from chronic insomnia. Although aware of the allegations against David, and the ongoing police hunt, he didn't believe the former, nor did he give a shit about the latter. There was little camaraderie between hackers and cops. When Eugene heard David's unusual request, he happily volunteered his services.

***

David stood alone in a decrepit factory. It had taken two days of scouting abandoned industrial spaces to find one that had a portal, and an additional twenty-four hours to fit-out the location.

The obsidian door glowed as the sun rose over it.

Steeling his nerves, David opened the door. Indifferent to the moonlit landscape that lay on the other side, he closed the door and waited.

"You escaped the paradox cell?"

David turned to face the Doorkeeper. "Not that it helped Celeste."

"Don't concern yourself over small matters. Not when larger concerns are looming." His piercing eyes regarded the obsidian door. "Why did you purposely draw my attention, David? Are you so keen to be re-imprisoned?"

David's phone beeped. He read the text message and grinned.

"Something amusing?"

"Did you notice what's in each corner of this building?"

The Doorkeeper scanned the factory. "Mirrors?"

"*Two-way* mirrors. Behind each one is a camera streaming live to the internet. Although they can't capture actual doors, they kept recording when you stepped your alien ass out of one. I just got confirmation."

David tossed his phone to the Doorkeeper, who plucked it out of the air and read the message. It was from Eugene: *Dude just materialized. WTF?*

"The internet is full of videos with special effects." The Doorkeeper threw the phone aside.

"That's why I also had my techy client attach a detailed explanation of the doors." David grinned. "If your job is to maintain the secret, I'd say you've failed spectacularly."

For one glorious moment, the unflappable Doorkeeper looked stunned. Shock quickly turned to anger, however, as he seized David by the throat and lifted him off his feet. "Do you have any idea what you've done?"

"Aside from exposing your incompetence?" David wheezed.

The Doorkeeper snarled as he hurled David into the air.

Feeling like a human Frisbee, David slammed into a brick wall. Blackness, spiked with blinding white dots, flooded his eyes. As he struggled to maintain consciousness, heavy hands lifted him to his feet.

"This is no time to sleep, David. This is the time to scream."

Exerting a vise-like pressure, the Doorkeeper squeezed David's shoulders, causing bones to crack. The pain was almost intolerable.

Using the pain as fuel, David head butted his tormentor with all the strength he could muster. The Doorkeeper roared as he flung David aside and hefted his cauterizing staff.

"Go ahead," David croaked. "Do it."

"That would be too easy."

The burning staff pressed into David's flesh, causing him to scream like a banshee.

"Pain is about to become your permanent friend." The Doorkeeper positioned the staff above David's legs. "Prepare to lose some limbs."

Before the amputation could occur, a hematite door appeared nearby. When it opened, a creature of light drifted out. Although roughly humanoid in shape and size, it shone so brightly that David couldn't make out its features.

The Doorkeeper bowed his head. "Greetings, High Councilor. You honor me with your presence."

The being responded with chiming sounds that reminded David of a whale song, only somehow more nuanced.

"I seek only to uphold the law," the Doorkeeper protested. "Blood must be spilled for what has transpired."

The being sang again, its melody taking on a deeper, darker tone.

"But this *human* committed the violations!" The Doorkeeper stabbed his finger in David's direction. "I assure you, in this matter I stand tall. I stand *blameless*."

The being of light flared as if enraged. Tentacles of light extended from its body, ensnaring the Doorkeeper where he stood.

"No!" The Doorkeeper tried using his staff to fend off the attack. It was to no avail. The blinding tentacles, ribbons of pure energy, drew the struggling Doorkeeper toward his master's bosom. When the two met, they jointly passed through the hematite door, which promptly disappeared.

Feeling strangely peaceful, David let his heavy eyelids close, not knowing whether he was surrendering to unconsciousness or death. Both loomed at the ready.

GOODBYES

Olivia pulled into the hospital parking lot and switched off the ignition. After checking she had her visitor ID, a tiny card that had taken her days to procure, she proceeded to the main building. Rain drizzled from the gray sky.

Security was tight, with large fences and multiple check-in stations. Olivia had to display her clearance ID on three separate occasions, each time having her name checked against a pre-registered list of approved visitors, before reaching David's room. He wasn't alone.

"Professor Milner?"

"Good to see you again, Officer Cho." Olivia shook Lisa's hand, ignoring the throbbing sensation beneath her bandaged palm.

"You've hurt yourself."

"Just a scratch."

"I didn't know you were a personal friend of Dr Druas."

The statement sounded accusatory. Olivia wasn't in the mood for games. "He means a great deal to me."

Both women studied David. He looked peaceful, like a slumbering child, despite being locked in a coma. Machines monitored his lifeless body.

"Have the doctors updated his prognosis?"

Lisa shook her head. "I'd give anything to question him."

Olivia had questions of her own. She wanted to ask David about the Doorkeeper and the factory footage. Most of all, she wanted to ask why the invocation had failed to work for her. Since she couldn't share these matters with Lisa, she offered the one piece of information that she *was* certain about: "David isn't a murderer."

"Off the record, I think you might be right. We discovered a few factual anomalies."

"Then why are you here guarding him?"

"I only came to visit." Lisa smiled. "Anything to get out of the office."

When Lisa departed shortly thereafter, Olivia sat beside David's bed and held his hand. It felt limp and heavy. "Your clients miss you. I found a talented psychologist to counsel them in your absence. They're in good hands."

For awhile they both resided in silence.

Reaching into her handbag, she withdrew her favorite book, *A New Earth*. Then, pausing to brush some hair off his forehead, she opened to a page at random and began reading to her slumbering, would-be son.

***

As the day grew late, Olivia decided it was time to leave the hospital.

"I'll be back tomorrow." She checked that David's blankets were neatly tucked, and kissed his forehead. "I'll even bring *To Kill A Mockingbird*. I know it's one of your favorites."

As she navigated through the sterile hospital, Olivia's thoughts drifted to happier times. But that was the past. Focusing on the present, she noticed the smell of pine disinfectant, the soft linoleum floor, the throbbing of her bandaged hand, the hum of an overhead light. They were small details, but small details gave birth to life.

Olivia stopped abruptly, suddenly doubting her eyes.

Several feet ahead of her, the corridor ended at a gothic-looking door, complete with carvings of gargoyles and imps. It radiated a soft luminescence.

I was blind, she thought, but now I see.

EPILOGUE

AWAKENING

The Doorkeeper newly assigned to Earth and its sister planets wore black. The color contrasted sharply to her white hair and skin. On Earth, many would label and shun her as an albino. On her home planet, although everyone was pale, the idea of shunning someone for being different was an odious concept.

Humans are a young species, she reminded herself. In their own words, they know not what they do.

The hospital she had come to visit looked small from a distance. It was a so-called secure building, with both medical staff and security personnel. Humans considered it virtually impregnable. She allowed herself a small smile before summoning a hematite door and transporting herself to one of its private rooms.

David Druas had been in a coma for nine months, the same time required for human gestation. The irony pleased her. It had taken the Doorkeeper all this time to get the permission for what she was about to do. That permission, a fragile thing, had almost been denied, but the Doorkeeper and her comrades had won it in the end.

Withdrawing an augmented healing stone from her pocket, she roused David from his coma.

***

Jolted awake, David found himself in a sterile room, with a pale woman standing over him.

"Where am I?" he asked.

"You are in a medical facility, David. You have been here for many months, trapped in a coma."

"Are you my doctor?"

"I am a Doorkeeper."

He recoiled. "Stay away from me!"

"Be at ease, David. I come bearing the gift of life. Unfortunately time is short so I must be brief." She glanced at the room's physical door. It was closed. "Your actions provoked considerable debate among the Council of Doorkeepers. Many demanded your death, for releasing information about the doors. However, since you withheld the actual invocation, they were unsuccessful."

"They?"

"Doorkeepers, like any diverse group, hold a range of opinions. Nevertheless, there are two primary factions. The disciplinarians and the moderates. Also known as the enforcers and the educators. Also known as the browns and the blacks."

"What do the browns believe?"

"They favor physical punishment and death for any breaches."

"And your faction?" David eyed her dress. "The blacks?"

"A significant number of my peers, including myself, believe the universe has a certain flow to it. When an individual discovers an invocation, many believe the discovery is *not* a random event."

"You're talking about fate."

"That is what you call it on this planet," she agreed. "Whether or not fate exists, our faction favors education over violence. None would—" She cocked her head to one side.

"What is it?" David asked.

"Someone is coming."

***

Padding through the hospital, the night nurse made her regular rounds. When she entered room B16, she found David Druas lying in a coma. A routine check of his vitals showed that everything was normal.

As she turned to leave the room, something odd caught her attention. The monitor switch – an alarm that alerted the nursing desk to any change in a patient's life signs – had been turned off. Bewildered, the nurse turned the switch back on and made a note of it in her logbook. The attending doctor would have to be informed.

Satisfied that everything else was in order, she left to check on her next patient. It was the beginning of another long, uneventful, night shift.

***

David felt the familiar jolt as his eyes fluttered open.

"The nurse is gone."

David sat upright. "In that case, perhaps you can tell me how your faction handles those who disclose invocations?"

"When diplomacy fails, as an absolute last resort, we would place such an individual in a contained environment."

"Like a coma?"

"No. A paradox cell."

"They're much the same." David sneered. "Like Doorkeepers, apparently."

"Not all cells are stark prisons. They can also be an endless, open space, teeming with flora and fauna. A paradise."

"Even paradise would sour after an eternity."

"Cells can be calibrated to allow for a normal lifespan, at the end of which, the traveler would be returned to his or her home planet and euthanized. But this rarely happens. Take Olivia Milner, for example."

David tensed. "What about her?"

"Shortly after you entered your coma, Olivia invoked the doors for herself. At that point, I made contact, warning her of the dangers and the need for secrecy."

"Did she comply?"

"Olivia's a smart woman, David. She understands discretion, despite encountering several worlds that would undoubtedly astound her colleagues."

"Research always meant more to her than renown."

"If you become a Doorkeeper, your role would be to observe and educate novices such as Olivia. You would also be at liberty to explore the entire universe. Think of the possibilities."

"And if I choose not to become a Doorkeeper?"

"Your body is damaged. Without Doorkeeper technology, you will slip back into a coma the moment I leave here."

David noticed the barred window. "The cops will be after me."

"We have the technology to alter your appearance. In any case, evading the authorities is not a problem for someone who can appear and disappear at will." Her lavender eyes held him. "I am offering you the opportunity to awaken to a new way of life, an experience like no other. The choice is yours."

Acknowledgements

Without my generous family, I'd be a starving writer. Thanks to Karola. Also George, Tina, Michael, Millie and Peter.

I'm incredibly grateful to the amazing team at Momentum, including Joel Naoum, Gareth Beal, and Anne Treasure. You've all done an amazing job.

Finally, thanks to Chris Ransom for the Latin translation, Ashley Capes for viewing an early draft, Counting Crows for inspiration via Colorblind, and Parramatta New Writers' Group for ongoing support and encouragement.